# Wrestling With Angels

# Wrestling With Angels

❋ ❋ ❋ ❋

By Daniel Gabriel

© 2015 by Daniel Gabriel
First Edition
Library of Congress Control Number: 2014950575
ISBN: 978-0-89823-334-6
e-ISBN: 978-0-89823-335-3

Cover design by Rolf Busch
Interior design by Daniel Arthur Shudlick
Author photo by Usry Alleyne, Inc.

The publication of *Wrestling with Angels* is made possible by the generous support of Minnesota State University Moorhead, The McKnight Foundation, the Dawson Family Endowment, and other contributors to New Rivers Press.

For copyright permission, please contact Frederick T. Courtright at 570-839-7477 or permdude@eclipse.net.

New Rivers Press is a nonprofit literary press associated with Minnesota State University Moorhead.

Alan Davis, Co-Director and Senior Editor
Suzzanne Kelley, Co-Director and Managing Editor
Kevin Carollo, MVP Poetry Coordinator
Vincent Reusch, MVP Prose Coordinator
Thom Tammaro, Poetry Editor
Nayt Rundquist, Assistant Production Editor
Wayne Gudmundson, Consultant

Publishing Interns:
Kjersti Maday, Kelly Mead, Mikaila Norman

*Wrestling with Angels* Book Team:
Jalen Burchill, Rachel Hieserich, Kirsten Lusty

∞ Printed in the USA on acid free, archival-grade paper.

*Wrestling with Angels* is distributed nationally by Small Press Distribution.

 New Rivers Press
c/o MSUM
1104 7th Avenue South
Moorhead, MN 56563
www.newriverspress.com

For Alex and Evan,
to add to the stories told 'round the fire . . .

# CONTENTS

## A-SIDE: BORDER STORIES

| | |
|---|---|
| Song for a Road Partner | 1 |
| In the House of Mr. Poo | 5 |
| The Road Goes Ever On | 19 |
| The Man on the Train | 31 |
| At the Forest's Edge | 43 |
| Dust to Dust | 47 |
| Unto Us, the Spoils | 61 |
| Waiting for the Void | 81 |
| Sometimes | 87 |

## B-SIDE: SHIFTING GEARS

| | |
|---|---|
| Jumping Off | 93 |
| Grandfather and the Fish-Glove | 97 |
| A Touch of the Word | 107 |
| The Boots of Alfred Bettingdorf | 113 |
| A Rocker's Guide to the History of the Future | 129 |
| The Watcher | 147 |
| The Devil Don't Sleep 'Til Sunrise | 153 |
| By the Terebinths of Mamre | 161 |

## BONUS TRACK

| | |
|---|---|
| DarkTime | 171 |

ACKNOWLEDGEMENTS
ABOUT THE AUTHOR

# A-Side: Border Stories

❀❀❀❀

# SONG FOR A ROAD PARTNER

❄ ❄ ❄ ❄

You wait four hours at the border, saying nothing
as the dust blows across from no-man's-land
and two robed officials
with beards flecked green from narcotic chew
tug at their falling turbans
as they poke and prod through your tiny pack.

You wait with the patience of uncertainty,
still fresh enough to dare
no judgment on the ways of the East.
Wait in your long, flower-riddled skirt
that will soon be tossed aside
as a worn-out symbol of a Western past.
Wait as night falls over
the tarmac trail to Herat while dancing stars
burst forth above the desert darkness,
speckling the inner eye with fireflies
and shooting down over the mountains
that bulk an ever darker blackness beyond the road.

Then in Herat—border city of the Afghan plateau—
you listen to the clop, clop, clopping
of the horses' hooves
as they pull the *tongas* home;
whipcracks sharp on the dust-strewn streets,
echoing off the compound walls that hide
your curtained sisters.
Gas lamps burn and fizzle
under shop awnings, sending flickered
glimpses of grain sacks, rusted hoes, and vast,
unexplained heaps of tattered cloth
like a hell for rag-and-bone merchants
condemned to flaunt their wares
in dark eternity.

The wind snaps across your face.
Dust spray whirls and dips on backhanded gusts,
blowing in off the Dasht-i-Margo
with the force of a thousand
years of undisturbed decay.
A bitter sting in the corner of the eyes,
the taste of gravestones on a thin-lipped mouth
until you pull your scarf
tight across your face
and all I can see are your eyes.
Still bright with fevered hope,
they cling to a daring
no road weariness could ever numb.
Stumbling over rutted paths that lead off
from the fizzing gas lamps into empty blackness
you touch the edge
of a mystery that leads forever East
and here you have just begun . . .

Would it make a difference if you knew?
If you saw in that blinded moment Margaret,
tossing in pain on the stained rubber sheet
of the cholera ward;
thick stench of the bucket beneath her bed
and birds nesting
in the cracked windows above her pallid stare.
If you saw your fever in a Kabul bed:
four days of delirium,
sweat-soaked sheets and uncounted trips on wobbly legs
down the corridor to squat, weaving like brush grass
to empty the pain and start again.
Then at last awake, that first step into the courtyard
and the dog bite sharp and sudden on your heel.
Horse needles at the hospital
and no rabies serum in all Afghanistan.

Would your feet turn aside
from the three a.m. departure for the Bamiyan jeep
and the long, twisting ascent
through crannies and defiles in the Hindu Kush,
riding for the sky?
And the valley—
set in green isolation, encircled by snows
and the silent, looming Buddha figures left
by forgotten caravans of silk—
would you pass that by?

Would it stop you if you knew
the color of Band-i-Amir?
Saw the unsullied blue of the spring-fed lakes
so deep that the sky itself bleeds down
and coats the surface of the waveless chain?
If you saw us stumbling, lost and hatless,

as we follow the mirage curve of the lake chain
out into the sunbeaten desert
and you so small inside the folds of an Afghan robe . . .

Later . . .
on our *caravanserai* bed you strike a tiny fire
inside the pipe and hold it close,
eyes lit from below and bright with the dream of passage.
The weeks dissolve beneath the flame
and the hard roads of Afghanistan curl
into the black pellet of soft resin and drift
off into the night sky
where stars explode and fall;
each one the end of another's forgotten dreams.

But your eyes remain
behind the flame's extinction,
sparks to light the pathway on—
and mirrors of the lure
    that first infected me with love.

# IN THE HOUSE OF MR. POO

✿ ✿ ✿ ✿

ON THE MORNING AFTER THE new moon, there were no lodgers in the house of Mr. Poo. There was a body under the back steps, but the body was dead, and had never lodged in any formal sense with Mr. Poo. It had washed up on the beach sometime during the night and been removed from public view by Mrs. Poo, a wiry, greying woman of great age and determination.

At first Mr. Poo had been inclined to leave the body where it was, along the fringe of sand, and give the whole matter over to the authorities. Mr. Poo was not given to extraordinary exertions. He had stood on the sand, musing in an unsettled way about the proper fate for a washed-up European body—particularly that of an adolescent, unknown to the island—when Mrs. Poo had pointed out the red, twisted markings on the boy's neck that indicated death by more deliberate means.

Mr. Poo had scratched at his stomach and spat a line of betel juice onto the sand. There could be no further talk of involving the authorities. The current climate of sentiment against the Chinese ensured that the very knowledge of a murdered European on the island (for what else could the neck markings mean?) would be taken as a sign of criminal infiltration by the family Poo.

Rumblings had been growing of late on the island—wild tales of tong war and drug-running that bore less relation to the quiet, settled world of the landlords Poo than to the last set of martial arts films imported from Hong Kong and shown against a sheet hung between two trees outside Suvendra's grocery store and bicycle repair. There were no other Chinese on the island with whom the Poos might have initiated such a tong war. Indeed, the nearest Chinese community of size was on the mainland at Hat Yai, and neither of the Poos had been there since the war. But it was the very irrationality of the claims that gave them credence, as it matched the islanders' growing confusion over their own expendability in the combat with modern market forces.

Still, rumblings or not, the body was there. Well out of sight from the house, or any passersby, but there nonetheless. It was evident that something must be done. Mr. Poo announced as much to his wife and then, with a yawn, decided to think matters over properly, and retired to the wooden platform under the shaded verandah of the house.

Mrs. Poo listened submissively to her husband's advice and then, after he padded off, dragged the body with great effort between two garden hoes up off the beach, across the patchy yard littered with browning palm fronds and an upturned dugout canoe, to the steps behind the house, where she stowed it carefully out of sight beneath two gunny sacks and a length of tarpaulin.

Mr. Poo knew nothing of this. He lay, as was his wont, lengthways on the wooden platform and watched the swell and dip of the waves that dodged past the western end of the reef and slid safely home to die on the shores of his beach.

Mr. Poo was a quiet, elderly fellow with a scalp so bald that the isolated tufts of white hair merely accented its nakedness. Left to himself, he might not move for hours, or even days, but in company he was a very smiley man. It was difficult to tell if he had any teeth even when he smiled, as his mouth held the clotted bloodstained mess that marked the final stages of betel nut addiction.

It was a happy, vacant smile, as big as Mr. Poo was small, though he possessed a potbelly of which he was enormously proud. He lay then, on the morning after the new moon, rubbing his belly affectionately and not thinking about the dead body which had been dragged up the beach to rest behind his house. He was thinking instead about money, and the remote chance of getting any, and whether it was possible that Suvendra's credit ledger might ever be mislaid.

Mrs. Poo was working over the wash basin in the backyard with a dim sense of impending trouble, when the sound of voices came through the palm thickets along the path to town. They were European voices and her first thought, naturally, was of the body.

Mr. Poo's first thought was of lodgers and he patted his belly at the thought of business at hand. He sat up, yawning, and waited for the voices.

"I mean, you can't just say, 'he understood,' can you? I mean, he might have understood a bit, or a lot, or—Hello, here's someone now. Hello? Have you got any rooms here? Rooms? Beds?"

The speaker was a fair, curly-haired boy with a permanently raw, sunburned forehead that spread redness like a stain across his face. That he was Australian, Mr. Poo knew, for he had heard the accent several times before. But usually it was accompanied by a swagger and a backslap, not the short, mincing steps of the boy before him.

Mr. Poo smiled helpfully, revealing his gash of clotted crimson. His English was sketchy, but here, without doubt, were lodgers.

"See what I mean now?" The curly boy turned to his partner. "I can't tell if he's understood, can you?" He looked again at Mr. Poo and shaped his words unnaturally on his lips. "Rooms?" he said. "Beds? Sleep?"

Mr. Poo nodded and smiled.

"Good God, can't he do anything but display his horrible gums? Beds! Sleep!" The Aussie laid his head on his palm as a hint.

His partner—a slim, dark Maltese with calf eyes and a Cheshire smile—laid a hand on the curly boy's arm. "There," he said softly. "It don't do to look too anxious."

Mr. Poo stood up, yawned, fumbled on a hook for some keys, and shuffled off around to the back of the house. The newcomers followed.

Mr. Poo led them up the back steps and pointed into a small room tucked under the eaves. He was smiling as widely as possible, in a vain effort at entrepreneurial allurement. There were a number of debts due in town and the last of the Poos' ready cash had been expended the week previous in a *mah jongg* game on the public square.

"He's got a canoe," said the sunburned Australian, peeking over his shoulder. "Did you see that? The dugout?"

"Too small."

"How can you be so sure? I heard once about—"

"Later. He wants us inside."

"But still, we can't rule out . . ."

Whatever else he said was lost inside the room. From her squatting position beside the outdoor wash basin, Mrs. Poo watched and wondered in her slow, steady way. It was too late to move the body now, but she could find no reason to think that its presence was known, or that its resting place was anything but secure. She would have to tell her husband, she realized, but later. He would not be pleased.

For one awful moment, the thought flitted through the mind of Mrs. Poo that the two lodgers had come to look for their missing European friend, but she set it carefully aside, along with a well-wrung pair of Mr. Poo's trousers, and took up something new. Trouble visited often enough without one beckoning it in from across the road.

※※

The sun had fallen onto the sea by the time the lodgers re-emerged from their room. Through the rift in the cloudbank over the outer islands, it shot its final shafts of light and lay dying in a pool of its own red afterglow. Mr. Poo lay on his platform, resting his head on a wooden four-by-four with a look of obvious contentment. The bare, polished wood seemed to have shaped the naked head to itself—flattening and squaring it off with the precision of a carpenter's plane.

The sunburned boy was talking. ". . . a couple days' supplies and a compass. If we're not out too long . . ."

"It's too small." Even when the Maltese spoke he held the smile on his face: clean, white, and sharp, like the edge of a surgeon's gown. And, like the gown, a sterile, unoffending cover for the work at hand.

Mr. Poo watched the pair with a sleepy eye. They moved under the covered verandah and sent the cat slinking into the trees.

"If it's so bloody small, what do you fancy doing? Sitting 'round here 'til somebody turns up with the rope and our descriptions on a police list?" The Aussie's voice rose as it finished.

The Maltese's eyes flicked to Mr. Poo and back. "Nobody's going to turn up," he said. "The only person who could have done us was Billy, and he's been shark supper long since by now."

"God, I hope so." The boy shook his curls. "I never did fancy him and his fertile-smelling little females. He was too bloody young, anyways."

The sun dipped out of sight and the red band across the sky softened.

"We could do a trial run in the canoe at least," said the curly boy. "I mean, what's the hurt?" He threw an endearing look at his friend.

Mr. Poo yawned and nestled his shoulders into the edge of the board.

The Maltese followed his movements. "Tomorrow we ask about boats," he said. "Casually, mind. Casually."

❁ ❁

Mrs. Poo waited until her husband had tossed the last bits of rice to the cat and set down his chopsticks before she told him about the location of the body. She took the obligatory beating without complaint (and, for his part, Mr. Poo administered it with a practiced lack of effort).

It was not Mr. Poo's habit to discuss matters of business with his wife, but after the beating, when she was serving his nightly tea, he announced that the Europeans must leave. To Mrs. Poo, nothing could have pointed out the danger of their situation more clearly. To turn lodgers away!

It was not only the lodgers that must go, explained Mr. Poo. The body must follow as well, but carefully, for should it wash up elsewhere along the fringe of beach, it might yet be linked to the house of Mr. Poo and the welcome to Europeans accorded therein.

As a temporary measure, the Poos crept out that evening and, under the cover of darkness, managed to dig a shallow trench alongside the upturned dugout and roll the body into it. Already there was a putrid, cloying smell to the flesh. They laid palm fronds over the spot where they had dug, imitating the scattered pattern of downed fronds found along the length of beach. Then they put the canoe back on top of the spot.

It was not a particularly good job, but it would have to do. By the end even Mr. Poo was gasping and wet with sweat.

Late in the night, a faint sliver of moon sliced the building clouds over the sleeping household, but only the cat—awake and stalking—was truly at peace.

In the morning, the two lodgers appeared on the verandah for their breakfast. After an unusually spirited session of bargaining, in which Mrs. Poo found herself agreeing to supply an extra egg and two cups of coffee at no additional cost (condensed milk available only by prior arrangement), the Maltese inquired in a soft, phlegmatic voice about the availability of boats.

Mr. Poo spat a thin stream of betel nut onto the ground and considered pretending he didn't understand. The Maltese had a smile like a cat preening his whiskers. His eyes seemed to focus everywhere at once. Indecision, felt Mr. Poo, was the best line of defense. He prevaricated.

"What's the bloody point?" said the curly boy. "He don't know nothing. Let's just point at the sodding canoe and be done with it."

His friend patted his arm, attempting to calm him. "Don't rush him," he said. "He is thinking. That is good."

Mr. Poo, who had decided he would fall asleep, twitched his feet twice and was still.

"Thinking! Bollocks." The Aussie stood up and moved towards the canoe, bringing Mr. Poo upright with an unexpected quickness.

"How about this one?" said the Aussie, pointing.

Mr. Poo waddled over and stood between the two Europeans and the canoe. With a heavy sadness he shook his head, indicating with hand gestures, brow furrows, and vague, unexplained hunchings of his shoulders that the boat in question was plainly not adequate. It had not been used in years.

"I don't believe him," said the Aussie. "There's a smell of dead fish still on it now."

Mrs. Poo watched from the back of the house.

The Maltese studied Mr. Poo and then, ever smiling, turned with the suddenness of a cat pouncing and looked at Mrs. Poo. She withdrew abruptly into the shadows.

The voices went on outside the house for nearly an hour. Mrs. Poo lit three sticks of incense in front of the household Buddha and brought out a lukewarm cola drink to each of the three men.

Some banknotes were being pressed into the hand of Mr. Poo. He nodded very, very slowly and announced that he would ask in town.

The cat was sniffing at the dugout. Mrs. Poo kicked it away.

❈ ❈

A day went by. Nothing happened.

The moon grew larger.

On the second day Mr. Poo went into town. In his absence, Mrs. Poo was cajoled into washing several of the Australian's shirts and then, after she had spread them in a line to dry, was saddled further with a smelly lump of undershorts and soiled handkerchiefs handed over by the Maltese. She worked without complaint. She knew no other way. But when she had carefully set down the folded stack of clean laundry and was chastised for not ironing the handkerchiefs, a dim, unfocused resentment began to coalesce in the placid mind of Mrs. Poo.

Late in the afternoon her husband returned on his bicycle, wobbling across the wooden catwalk over the river and easing to a halt next to Mrs. Poo's outdoor oven. His shirt was wet and dark under his arms and sweat drops dangled like earrings from the bottoms of his naked ears.

He was carrying a bag. There had been trouble in town, he said. Three youths had leapt at him as he bicycled past, shouting "chinky, chinky" and planting *kung-fu* kicks on Mr. Poo's posterior until he toppled and fell in the dirt.

It was most definitely a time to lie low. Mr. Poo unhitched the bag from the handlebars with a dull, morose look clinging to his hairless face like a mask.

The Europeans were waiting on the verandah. The items in the bag were laid out for their inspection: six tins of fish, four cans of condensed milk, a loaf of flat, hard bread, and a crude schoolboy's compass with a picture of the king on the reverse.

Mr. Poo looked weary.

"And the boat?" said the Aussie, leaning in close to Mr. Poo. "What about the boat?"

Mr. Poo exposed his gums.

The Aussie pulled at his curly hair and swore. "Every day we wait's an invitation to disaster," he said. "Why are we even messing about with these bloody fools? All it takes is questions in the right places and we're had, we are."

"Your agitation is unseemly," said the Maltese.

"Unseemly, my arse." The red stain of sunburn deepened on the Aussie's face. "Why don't we just do these two in and be done with it? Who'd miss two worthless old chinks anyway?"

The Maltese's stare had gone cold as ice water and under it, the Aussie softened and went quiet. "There's a lot you don't see, old cock," said the Maltese. "Do you suppose this island is so big that we wouldn't be remembered? We gain nothing by removing these two. It's a boat we want and here at hand we have a go-between to get it. I don't fancy putting to sea in that rotting hulk of a dugout if I can help it, do you?" He looked at Mr. Poo. "The boat, my friend. Where is the boat?"

There was no boat, explained Mr. Poo. Except for the twice-weekly ferry to Ko Samui. Leaving next Friday, he went on. Tickets still available.

He crinkled his eyes in hopeful good humor and then, blinking, fell back with a thud against one of the pillars of the verandah. The Aussie stood over him, flexing his hand to strike again. "I ought to ram that bloody mess you chew right down your throat. You're too dumb for words, you are."

The Maltese hissed once and the Aussie fell silent. His hand continued to twitch, like a man with a nervous tic. Slowly, Mr. Poo pulled himself upright and sat down on his wooden platform. Mrs. Poo rose from behind her oven and edged over towards her man.

The Aussie's nostrils flared at the movement and he rammed his fist through the bamboo edging along the verandah's roof. "That's for the both of you," he said. "I'm fed up with waiting." He turned away and stomped off to their tiny room where he could be heard banging something on the inside wall.

The Maltese leaned back where he sat and whispered to Mr. Poo. "Not good enough," he said. "We must have a boat. Tomorrow." His smile stretched narrow and tight across his face. "It will be better for you." He looked across at Mrs. Poo, paralyzed against the near wall of the house. "It will be better for her."

Mr. Poo spat a juicy, blood-red stream at the lurking cat. It screeched and dashed off, reaching up to scratch and nibble at the overturned dugout canoe.

The Maltese's eyes followed it.

Winds came in the night, whistling fear through the palm trees and driving heavy, hanging clouds before them onto the sea. No stars were visible, but just near dawn a fissure appeared in the cloudbank and a slice of moon threw a trail across the rocking waves beyond the reef.

Mr. Poo went again to town.

In his absence, Mrs. Poo busied herself in the house, leaving the Europeans to stalk the beach: up and down, up and down, until it might have been an army that had sullied the yielding sand.

Twice she had come out of the house to find the Maltese slinking at right angles to the canoe, measuring it—and her—with the inner fire of his cat's-eye stare.

Again she lit her three incense sticks, but the middle one kept going out, flickering and guttering no matter how many matches she applied.

Sometime about noon the Maltese appeared at the open window of the house, hissing in a faint, sibilant whisper that drew Mrs. Poo unwillingly towards its sound.

"Fresh water," said the Maltese. "We shall need fresh water."

Mrs. Poo pretended not to understand.

"Give me the container." The Maltese's eyes were bright and gleaming. "There in the corner. The container. I will pay you well." He exhibited the folded corner of a wad of bills, gesturing impatiently at a silver plated urn resting against the inner wall. Mrs. Poo, who had almost decided to give him whatever it would take to make him go away, hesitated at the sight of the money. Finances were not her domain. And the container, an heirloom from Canton, was not replaceable.

The Maltese extended the bills slyly with one hand, turning

them so that the zeros were visible even in the gloom of the room's interior.

Mouse-like, Mrs. Poo stepped forward, sniffing at the promised fortune. Heirloom or not, the opportunity to clear the debts in town could scarcely be overlooked.

The Maltese's grin expanded and then, in the long moment of transfer, as he received the heavy water container and left Mrs. Poo with the water-soaked bundle of obsolete Laotian notes, it disappeared altogether.

Later it would return.

And later still, Mrs. Poo would realize her mistake. The beating would be the least of it.

In the afternoon, the lodgers slept and Mrs. Poo devised a plan.

When Mr. Poo returned home wearing his sweat earrings and a look of profound melancholia, Mrs. Poo took him aside. It took quite a time to reveal her plan, for it was necessary that Mr. Poo believe himself to be its author. When this was accomplished Mrs. Poo withdrew, watching from a window as Mr. Poo stumped across the fringe of scrub and sand to the spot where the lodgers stood looking out over the reef and the waves beyond.

Tomorrow, he would say to them. Tomorrow you shall have a boat. But you must depart with the moon—or the tide shall bring you down on the rocks of the reef.

From the house she watched him speaking this, proud of her man. She could see the red one jumping about and throwing stones in the air. He pumped her husband's hand and hugged his friend. But the black one was silent, nodding and watching as if from a great interior distance.

Through the night the Poos worked. Again the winds were heavy, disturbing the trees so they rustled like gossiping neighbors spreading slander about things they hardly knew. But clouds blew in with the winds, blanking the sky and covering all deeds done in the darkness.

When Mrs. Poo brought breakfast to the lodgers' room they were already awake and waiting, though dawn was hours away.

"It's the old bat," said the red one through the door. He opened it. "She's brought a bit of brekky. Just hope I can eat."

A sibilant voice responded, "You must. Our journey will be long." His eyes flicked over Mrs. Poo. She held her face rigid and expressionless. "Poor dumb creature," said the Maltese.

"Oh, I don't know," said his friend. "She's got enough wit to keep her trap shut." He was stuffing bits of egg into the corner of his mouth.

"The cat has more initiative than these two."

Mrs. Poo nodded silently and withdrew.

A few moments later the lodgers emerged. Mr. Poo was waiting for them on the patch of beach outside the house. There was an argument over the bill. The Aussie's demand that change be given in Malaysian coins was turned away with the customary "no change" shrug, which led to a general unwillingness on the part of the lodgers to pay anything at all, and a stiff right arm that caught Mr. Poo squarely on the shoulder. He accepted the few proffered notes sadly, remembering the good years before the wars, when all the zeros meant something and Laotian mah jongg dens had been a solace worth seeking. Then he unveiled the boat. It was the dugout canoe.

The sight of it brought further protests and a burst of interaction between the two lodgers that neither of the Poos could understand. The canoe bobbed in the shallow waters along the shoreline, low and dim under the cloud cover.

"Still a hell of a smell to it," said the curly-haired boy.

"It's only rotten fish," said the Maltese. "We shan't even notice it in the water."

Mr. Poo stepped forward to assist in the loading of stores and found himself wading from boat to shore and back again as the two Europeans issued orders from the beach. Mrs. Poo, with her customary meekness, produced two cardboard boxes, a rarity on the island, and offered one to the red-faced Australian as protection for the exposed container of water.

He gestured for her to put the container inside the canoe and then, with a final stone flung at the watching cat, relieved himself on the beach and began to roll up his pants.

The Poos wrestled the heavy box out into the tide and set it carefully in the middle of the canoe. In the dim light of the coming day, Mrs. Poo's face was shadowed and long. She was remembering Canton and the day she'd been given the urn.

Finally, the lodgers waded out and climbed aboard, settling themselves with care and curses into the shallow bottom. Paddles were handed out and with a final wave to the Poos, the red, curly-haired boy pointed north, away from Malaysia, and shouted "Bangkok! We go to Bangkok!"

Mr. Poo's gums yawned cavernously.

The canoe began to bob and move as the two Europeans adapted to each other's rhythm. The Maltese called cadence. The boat got smaller and smaller until even the gleam in the Maltese's eyes was invisible as he looked back, one last time.

Mrs. Poo moved up to stand next to her husband and as she did, she felt a warm slink of cat fur along her leg. She looked down at the cat and allowed herself a faint smile of familiarity. The family Poo stood there on the shoreline as the boat departed and the winds blew in from the north. The tiny canoe bobbed and dipped on the waves and, as it breasted the reef to move out into the higher seas, it seemed to sink almost imperceptibly under its unaccustomed weight.

The heavy clouds rumbled and split, cut by the scythe of the quarter moon and bleeding a line of light down over the bobbing boat. One of the figures in the boat—ant-like now and almost invisible to Mrs. Poo—stood up suddenly and a wave broke over the side.

Mrs. Poo turned away. It would be only time before the bottom-heavy keel would rend apart and disgorge its cargo. Only time before the three of them would float together on the all-accepting sea. She bent with effort over the second cardboard box, feeling the water slosh inside the silver-plated urn and wondering how long the jug of sea water she'd loaded into the box in the canoe would float.

Mr. Poo expelled betel nut on the ground and the light spatter of red was like blood freshly spilled in the light of the new day.

There were no lodgers in the house of Mr. Poo.

# THE ROAD GOES EVER ON

❋ ❋ ❋ ❋

A STEADY RUNNEL OF WATER fell onto the boy's shoulder, soaking through the fabric of his denim jacket. He shifted back and forth, trying without success to shelter himself in the lee of a faded highway sign. The rain continued to fall.

Gradually, he became aware of a dark smudge at the road's horizon. It expanded with the passing seconds to reveal a car. His spirits rose, and with them, his thumb. His feet danced. The car came on in a rush and then, in a flurry of wetness, sped past, leaving only a fine mist suspended in the air, which dissolved quickly earthwards.

The boy sat down. "So much for taking the road less traveled by." He adjusted himself again atop the battered cloth bag that lay propped along the base of the half-sheltering sign.

The day stretched on. Cars began as distant specks, approached, and passed. Only the rain ceased, until it too was but a memory of the long day's wait.

The boy stretched restlessly and blinked his eyes. In the distance, another speck appeared. This one grew more slowly until at last it resolved itself into the figure of a man. At first the boy could make out only the most obvious details: baggy brown suit, cloth cap pulled down over the eyes, and a curious shuffling gait that gave the impression of both an indomitable willingness to continue and a strong desire to stop.

The figure drew near. The boy could see now the shabbiness of the suit, the etched-deep lines hidden beneath the cap. Cracked lips parted in two bristly cheeks: "'Low, boy. Been here long?"

"Since last night. Just can't seem to slow anybody down."

"Know the feeling all too well." The man's head wagged up and down. "I been walking ever since K.C., and I guess I'll just have to keep to it."

"You're welcome to hang on here. I can't do any worse than I have been."

The older man shifted where he stood, grimacing slightly. His left shoe hung open, exposing a piece of tattered sock. "Well," he said, "I 'preciate that, but I guess I'll just keep walking. Least I end up somewhere different."

He hitched his shoulders and the boy could see a small bundle protruding from under the folds of his suit coat.

"You a bindle stiff?" the boy asked.

The old man's eyes narrowed. "Now where'd you learn a word like that?"

"Read it, I guess." The boy's face flushed.

"Bindle stiff." The old man patted at his bundle. "That's me all right. Last of them just about. Ain't like the old days." He spat on the ground. "No sir. Freights're just about played out. Ain't like the old days. No sir."

He turned down the road, still shaking his head.

The boy called after him. "Hey mister, mind if I walk along? I'm getting kind of bored just sitting here."

The old man stopped and looked back. His tongue licked out at his lower lip. "Well . . . no harm in it I can see. Come along, boy." He turned again and trudged steadily on.

The boy reached down to grab his bag and settled it under his jacket like he'd seen the old man do. Then he hustled down the road 'til he caught up to the stooped, shuffling figure. He fell in step.

The road stretched out before them to where the day's last light lay dying in the distance.

❦ ❦

They were jailed in Salt Lake City. The old man had recommended it. "They only keep you for the weekend," he'd said. "Shower and a bed, three meals a day. All for free—can't beat that."

The boy had been silent.

Now he was frightened. He paced the cell: five steps up, turn, five steps back. Five steps up . . .

"Boy, whyn't you rest your bones?" said the old man. "That's the point of it."

"What if they don't let us go on Monday?"

The old man laughed, or tried to. He ended by coughing: a deep, racking cough that shook his frame 'til he spat into the bucket in the corner. "Boy," he said, his voice a rasp. "Boy, they don't want to keep us. Costs them money. Old judge'll frown down from his high chair . . ."

The boy laughed at the old man's imitation of the frowning judge.

"He'll frown down and say, 'You two keep on moving west. Salt Lake City got no place for vagrants.'" The old man sat back and coughed again. "I guarantee it. He done said it to me three, four times already."

The boy wrapped his hands around the steel bars of the door and looked down the corridor. "I've never been caged up like this before."

"You're talking nonsense. You been caged ever' day of your life." The old man opened one eye and peered up at the boy. "Ain't that why you're walking the line?"

"I don't know . . ." The boy stared down the corridor towards the outside door. "I don't know . . ."

Monday morning they went up to court. The clerk droned through his report and they were officially charged with vagrancy. Then the judge adjusted his bifocals and leaned down to see where the two defendants stood. "Court suspends further sentence," he said. "Provided the defendants depart these premises immediately upon release." He took off his glasses and frowned. "Salt Lake City has no place for vagrants." He pounded his gavel and called out, "Next case."

The vagrants departed.

❊ ❊

A trucker picked them up on Route 80. They scrambled into the cab and got settled. "Where you bound for?" he said.

"California," said the boy, yelling over the noise of the engine. He lay up on the sleeping area behind the seats.

The trucker looked the two of them over. He was a large man with a splotchy face and a green snake tattooed on his right arm. He ran his way up through the gears and when the rig was sailing smoothly, spoke again. "You both going to the same place?"

"Nope," the old man said. "I'm just going to California. Boy here's going to the Promised Land."

The trucker guffawed. He glanced back at the boy. "First time out, eh?" He took out a pack of cigarettes and the two men lit up. The boy declined.

The road ran level—dead flat, straight ahead—through the salt flats of western Utah. The shimmering haze of mirage ascended from the desert floor like smoke from a day-old fire. The boy yawned. The smell of diesel and the rocking of the cab made him sleepy and he put his head down on his pack.

Voices droned from the front. He slept.

He woke with a start. The truck was idling at a stop sign, and lights—a shifting profusion of lights—blinked and flashed their color-coded messages of invitation in all directions. He sat up and tried to clear his head. Through the side window of the cab he watched the lights run through their paces. BEER, said one, blinking on and off... GO GO GO ... ALL NIGHT ... a neon poker hand flashed and disappeared.

The old man looked back and grinned. "Reno," he said. "This here's where we get out."

The boy clambered down from the cab of the truck and stood in the street, still groggy and grasping at his pack.

The trucker leaned over and waved good-bye. "You watch out for that Promised Land," he said. "They don't keep 'em." His right arm pulled the cab door shut and left the boy with a final image of the tattooed snake writhing on his arm.

They settled their bundles under their coats and headed west past the blinking invitations. The old man's tongue licked over his lips. "You wouldn't have the price of a bottle, would you boy?"

❈ ❈

Even without the hangover, California was different right from the start. For one thing, there was a border: a real border with men in uniforms and walkie-talkies. The tall cowboy they were riding with had to pull his pickup over to the side of the road. They all got out. Two officials poked about in the back of the truck and then asked in a rapid singsong, "Are you carrying any firearms, fresh fruit, or liquor?" They all shook their heads. "Cigarettes, more than two hundred?" Again their heads wagged.

The officials looked at each other. The younger of the two waved his hand at the cowboy. "Okay, you can go." They got back in the pickup.

"Just a minute." The older official put his hands onto the window frame and looked in at the old man. "Old-timer, don't I know you from somewheres?"

The old man kept his head lowered, so that the official was staring at the top of his cap. "No, sir. Don't believe so."

The official stood there for a minute, considering. He dipped his head down and looked at the boy in the middle of the seat. The boy smiled. The official straightened up and backed away.

The cowboy put a new chaw of tobacco in his mouth and pulled back onto the road. He had grey eyes and a tight-set chin.

His belt buckle showed a tomahawk and a rifle crossed like an X. He never spoke.

At the top of the pass, he dropped them off and grunted a good-bye.

The boy stretched and fidgeted on the roadside, while the old man sat watching him with just the hint of a smile. "What do you think of it, boy? This here's California."

The boy kicked at stones on the road's shoulder. "I guess I expected something different."

"Well," said the old man, "this is the Donner Pass. All downhill from here. Yessir," he chuckled, "all downhill from here." He took out a sack of tobacco and began to roll a cigarette.

The boy threw stones at the nearest trees.

When the old man's cigarette was lit, he spoke again. "Heading somewhere in particular?" He raised one eyebrow. "Or just heading?"

The boy stopped throwing. "Just heading, I guess. I got an address to look up in San Francisco, but it's no big deal." He looked down at the man. "How about you?"

"Frisco'll do me just fine. I got some money to collect."

They studied each other. The old man spoke. "When you going back East?"

The boy shrugged. "Whenever," he said. "Maybe never."

"You done let go the lifeline, eh?" The old man laughed, and again it turned to coughing—a harsh wheeze that made the boy's chest hurt.

When it stopped, the boy tried to smile. "I don't know. I guess. What do you mean?"

The old man stood up and walked around the packs, holding his chest. He spat with difficulty. "The lifeline," he said, pulling an invisible line behind him. "That's what you're holding when you know you're going back—to a family . . . or a job . . . or anything at all." He wiggled the imaginary line. "So long's you're dragging that, you'll never be free. You see what I mean? It's always got hold of you." He looked at the boy—and then beyond. "Here's a ride."

They turned and waggled their thumbs at a cherry-red Camaro burning rubber around the bend.

"My name's Bobby," said the blond boy behind the wheel. "Bobby Blue from San Berdoo." He flashed a quick smile, teeth white against the deep tan of his skin. He wore a t-shirt with a surfboard emblem sewn onto the sleeve. They were hardly settled into their seats, but already the Camaro was doing 50 . . . 60 . . . 65. The boy watched the speedometer climb.

"Been this way before, have you?" said the old man.

"Oh yeah," said Bobby with a yell. "Many times."

"Quite a drop, other side of the pass."

Bobby laughed. "Don't I know it." 70 . . . 75.

The height of the pass was just ahead. He dropped his foot off the accelerator and turned off the engine. Then he looked at the boy in the back seat and flashed another grin.

They hit the crest at 60 and the car rolled silently down the other side. In front of them the road descended in curves into the far distance.

It was all so smooth and silent. The boy rested his chin on the back of the seat in front of him and drifted with the roadside hypnosis. The soft whoosh of the tires was the only sound. Beyond the window, the world opened out like a view from the stars: the road a grey, sinuous curl through the thickets of trees. They wove in time to the tires' whooshing; curl left, curve right, curl left . . . The trees whizzed faster, faster 'til they blurred and the whoosh was a whine. The boy's trance ended and he glanced at the driver.

The muscles on Bobby Blue's arms stood out like knots on a rope. He looked neither right nor left, just held a long unblinking stare on the road ahead as those knotted muscle-cords twisted the wheel through the quickening curves.

The speedometer read 95 and climbing. On Bobby's face was a vast, ecstatic smile, fixed and white against his skin.

100 . . . 105 . . .

They could feel the air streams pushing against them now. A lone car loomed, was passed, disappeared. They descended in silence, dream-like, the car inscribing S-curves in its wake.

The old man never moved.

110 . . . 115 . . .

Down they went, their ears popping and burning, descending the pass, swooping like roadbed eagles on a tarmac sky. Eyes fixed . . . the trance heavy on their brains.

120 . . . 130 . . .

Bobby's eyes were glassy and bright. The veins on his forehead pumped with blood. His arms bulged.

Signs flashed by too fast to read.

The curves displayed a final helix, and the road, at last, began to level out.

At 140 the left front tire began to smoke. In one smooth motion Bobby's foot let go the clutch and tapped at the brake. They were in fourth gear at 130 now . . . his tapping continued, gently at first, then stronger and stronger as the smoking tire whined for relief. 120 . . . 105 . . . It exploded—like a rifle shot in muggy air—and the car jerked and twisted like a wounded beast.

In the back seat, the boy's mouth flapped in silent terror. His hands gripped the seat, white-knuckled, as the final seconds of life clicked by in slow motion before his eyes.

At the wheel, Bobby fought and bucked the veering auto. They swayed left, right, left . . . and then back right . . . shooting off the highway onto a rough line of dirt and smashing headlong into the protective barrier of sand at its end.

There was a sharp crack, thudding, and a momentary burst of horn as Bobby's chest bounced off the steering wheel. Then it was quiet.

For a moment, the boy felt nauseous. He wanted air; needed it. He fumbled open the back door and dragged himself out, knees wobbling as he gulped for breath.

In the driver's seat Bobby Blue was laughing uncontrollably. Wild, vibrant laughter from the pit of his stomach. He whooped and hollered and . . . then broke off.

Beside him, the old man lay face forward on the dashboard. The window above his head was cracked and a red smear opaqued its surface.

They dragged him out and laid him on the ground. He was unconscious, but his heart still beat. The boy put his denim jacket under the old man's head. Bobby went to look for water.

The boy sat watching the old man struggle to breathe. The lines in the old man's face stood out against his now-pale skin like reminders of the routes he'd traveled: a road map of his soul. Not a lifeline, for the old man had long since let that loose; but as the boy watched, he wondered if another kind of lifeline wasn't ebbing away. Blood still trickled from the wound on his forehead and the boy wiped it away with his sleeve.

The old man coughed; feebly at first, then with the gut-wrenching intensity that the boy had grown familiar with. He tried to roll over and failed. The boy bent over and soothed him until Bobby reappeared.

They poured water on his face and then, as he spluttered and blinked, offered it up to his lips. He coughed and drank and coughed again. They moved him under a tree and he sat up. For several minutes he sat wheezing for air. The gash on his forehead stopped oozing blood and began to swell. At last the old man opened his eyes and looked at the two of them from some deep distance outside their experience.

He focused on Bobby. "You're a damn fool," he said, and fell to coughing again.

It was dark by the time they hit Sacramento. None of them felt like talking. The Camaro still ran, but with balks and jerks, as if it realized how close their brush had been with the end of the road. Bobby squirmed in his seat and concentrated on events outside the car. The boy sat beside him, mute. Somehow he felt guilty, though he knew there was no reason he should.

He tried to pretend he was out of the car and walking the dark, unknown street beside them. Shops flashed by: shuttered, dark. Street lights reflected dim pools of light in the upper stories, where the shop owners and their tenants moved as shadows across the wall. Fragments of their lives were visible to the passing car: a mirror, a crucifix, a light bulb swinging naked.

No one walked on the street outside. Autos lined the curb. The boy imagined himself strolling, solitary, invisible to the people whose lives moved behind the windows of the tiny rooms. Block after block they went, the Camaro still struggling to regain its former verve.

At last Bobby nosed it in to a gas station, where the boy got out and stretched while Bobby filled the tank. The old man lay unmoving in the back.

The toilet was at the back of the building, just beyond a haphazard stack of discarded tires. Inside, a fluorescent light buzzed above stale green walls and unwashed fixtures. The odor of urine and chemicals clung to the air.

The boy relieved himself and stared vacantly into the mirror set in the empty towel rack. His face looked wind-burned and his eyes red. His hair was tousled and when he ran his hands through it they came away coated with the dust of the road. He wondered if he looked as old as he felt.

He bent over the sink, doused his face with water and wiped it on his sleeve. He went back outside.

They split up in San Francisco. The boy had slept from Sacramento all the way to Berkeley, waking only at a nudge from Bobby Blue, who nodded out the window.

"Bay Bridge," he said. "You'll be getting out on the other side."

The boy rubbed his eyes and tried to focus.

"Better wake the old man," said Bobby.

"No need." The old man's voice came from the back in a hoarse undertone. "I know where I am." He coughed once and was silent.

They came down off the bridge and Bobby rolled to a stop. "I head south from here."

The two riders got out.

"Hey, thanks," said the boy. "Thanks a lot."

The old man pulled his cap down firmly. "You may be a damn fool," he said to Bobby, "but I surely do appreciate that ride. You hear?"

Bobby's smile was quick and easy. "No sweat. We'll do it again sometime." He popped the clutch and the Camaro jerked southwards.

When it was gone, they shouldered their bags and walked toward the lights. The boy yawned. "Where are we?"

"Embarcadero," said the old man. "Know that address of yours, do you?"

"Haight Street," said the boy. "Somewhere near Golden Gate Park, I think."

"Might have guessed." The old man shuffled along in the same curious gait as when the boy had first seen him. If he was tired, he didn't show it. He cocked an eye at the boy. "You got a ways to walk, you know."

The boy yawned. "Just point me right and I'll get there. Right now I'm too beat to care."

They came to a corner and the old man stopped. "You carry on straight ahead," he said. "Till you get to Ashbury. Then go right. You'll have to ask again." He shifted his bag and spat onto the ground. "Me now, I'm going over to Mission. Got some mail to collect." He stuck out his hand. "You were a good old partner, boy."

The boy shook his hand solemnly. "You taught me a lot," he said. "I'll remember that lifeline."

The old man's cracked lips parted in a smile. "You'll be right. Long's you keep your nose turned to the road ahead—and let what's gone be gone."

The boy watched the old man shuffle to the corner and then on out of sight. He never looked back.

There was a flicker of neon in the distance straight ahead and the boy watched it from somewhere deep inside himself. Then he shifted his bundle under his coat and moved on up the street, whistling softly through his teeth.

# THE MAN ON THE TRAIN

❀ ❀ ❀ ❀

A FAT CUSTOMS OFFICER STOOD sniffing over my passport as the carriage rattled on in its descent. Then we were in Yugoslavia; the train leveled out and ran hard and fast into the narrow gorge of a river valley. His duties ended, the customs man inched his bulk through the crowded aisle back towards the bottle of plum brandy being passed in the rear of the car. The train went into a tunnel.

In the darkness, echoes rattled the length of the carriage. Out we came. A thin, weedy fellow with an enormous grin slicing through his face stood in the aisle, bracing himself against my seat. He looked surprised to see another westerner.

"Hel-lo!" he said, accenting the second syllable. "Ain't this train great? Just cutting along like nobody's business. Whoo!" The smile expanded across his face 'til I thought his cheeks would split.

"Sit down," I said. "I could do with some company." It had been weeks since I'd spoken English, beyond the occasional grunted phrase with one of my local contacts. "Where you coming from?"

He bounced into the seat beside me, wispy hair trickling down around his ears, his eyes small and bright behind his glasses. "You American?" he said.

"Born and bred. You?"

"Oregon. Near Portland. Say, we *are* in Yugoslavia now, right?"

I nodded.

For just a moment, that smile disappeared and he was serious. "We're out of Bulgaria for sure?"

"For sure. You dislike it all that much?"

"Oh man, if I could tell you—" He broke off and nudged me. "That official. That guy in the uniform back there. Who's he?"

"He's from the Bulgarian side. He's nothing here. Just along for the ride."

"You're sure?"

I was beginning to wonder. "What're you, a refugee?"

He broke into a whistling laugh, then stopped and looked over his shoulder. The fat man from customs was pulling hard on the plum brandy. My companion relaxed; there was that grin again, stretched all the way to the end of his jaw.

"Refugee?" He chuckled over it. "That's not so far off, man. Hey, listen—you going on to the Austrian border?"

"Beyond."

"Great." He shoved his pack underneath my seat. "I got to tell somebody, might as well be you. My name's William," he said. "William McGee."

"Ryder."

We shook hands.

As he settled himself, William tossed out, "Say, what is it you do, anyway?"

In my mind I saw the false bottom of my suitcase—and the Bibles that were no longer there. I thought of the people I'd left behind on this swing through Eastern Europe: pastors whose health had been permanently broken by torture and old women in head scarves and shawls who prayed through tears for the release of their grandchildren from state-run institutions. I ran my fingers across the outside of my coat pocket. I thought of the list it held, of the people who had "just disappeared."

I coughed mildly and said, "Literature distribution."

William gave a short laugh. "Literature, huh? Well, three

months ago I was *studying* literature—German Medieval—at Portland State."

He fumbled around for a moment and produced a package of cigarettes. "What did I know?" He grinned to himself. "But that was three months ago."

He took out a cigarette, lit it up, and leaned back in his seat. "Last week I was in Turkey," he said, exhaling upwards. "On a bus. Not a public bus—there was this English guy driving west from Kabul back to London, taking passengers and stuff. Mostly Aussies, a few Brits. I was the only American." He dragged again. "We trucked it straight through from eastern Turkey all the way to Istanbul." He paused and shook his head. "Lot of hostile Turks out there.

"By the time we got to Istanbul we were fed up with the country. Just wanted to get out. The Bulgarian Embassy told us we didn't need visas as long as we were just in transit. Great, I thought. One less expense. So let's see, Monday . . . no, Tuesday morning it was, we set off for the border. You know the stretch?" I nodded. His angular face returned the motion and he went on. "We stopped in Edirne for supper, so we didn't hit the frontier until after dark. The Turkish side was a breeze. On the Bulgarian side they did the usual searches—nothing very thorough, which was fortunate. Then the police asked to see passports. No problem 'til they got to mine.

"This hook-nosed guy with a scarred-up mouth looked it over, and then he kind of spat in my face: 'Visa,' he said. 'Visa. *Nix gut.*'

"I looked right back at the guy and said, 'What? Embassy say *no* visa.'

"He whined at me and shook his finger. 'Visa, visa.'

"I pointed to all the other passengers. 'No visa, no visa.'

"He sneered then, and I remember his rotting teeth. 'American,' he said. 'Visa.' Then he took my passport and got off the bus. I had to follow."

"Didn't anybody on the bus try to help out?"

He laughed, but it sounded forced. "What could they do?

The guy had my passport. Just before I got to the door the English driver took me aside and whispered, 'Look, they'll tell you to go back to Istanbul, sure as anything. Act as if you shall—be woeful and such. I'll run the bus on through customs and we'll pull off to the side of the road, just up a ways. Right? We'll wait one hour. If you can sneak through—somehow—we'll be there. If not . . .' He shrugged.

"I thought about being dumped out in Turkish no-man's-land in the middle of the night. I wasn't sure I even had enough money to get back to Istanbul. I told him I'd be there.

"'Right,' he said. 'But we can't wait forever, or the border guards'll get suspicious. And that I cannot have. One hour.'

"I got off the bus.

"The official hissed and howled while I hung my head and acted properly contrite. Finally, he waved the bus through. After it was gone, he gave me my passport and pointed me back towards Turkey."

William stubbed out his cigarette and stretched in his seat. He sneaked another glance around the train carriage. The bloated face of the official eyed the disappearing plum brandy with a visible hunger. The overhead lights brightened and dimmed erratically.

I thought about no-man's-lands that stretch between borders—sometimes inches, sometimes miles—where nothing but uniforms are safe, and then only if their color is the same as yours. "What did you do? That area's desolate. Edirne must be the nearest town and that's thirty miles away."

He lit another cigarette and blew smoke rings at the ceiling. "I put on my pack and walked back into the darkness. I only went a couple hundred yards or so, then I dropped off the road into this empty field and skirted across it 'til I figured I was out of sight. The border was close, but distance is deceptive after dark. Who knew how close? And who knew where the guards were or what they'd do if they spotted a shadowy figure sneaking through the night? They all carried machine guns, and I figured they wouldn't think twice about a little extra target practice. I mean, you can imagine what I was thinking."

I could.

William went on. I thought I noticed a tremble in his voice, but perhaps it was only the movement of the train. "Oh, was I cautious. Way off to the right was a bit of light that marked the border post and I watched that with every step I took. I went slow and careful, but even so it was hard going. The ground was rocky, uneven. My biggest fear—besides machine guns—was that I'd fall into a pit or something. Heaven knows when I'd ever be found.

"Then I spotted another light, not too far beyond the border. It was the bus, and that gave me new hope.

"When I got a little closer I figured I'd better keep low, so I started to crawl. That damn pack kept slipping off my back. I crawled . . . and I crawled . . . and every now and then I stopped to listen.

"Then I hit the border. It was barbed wire—thick, triple strands, almost a solid wall of wire, ten feet high. I tried climbing, but it was too wobbly and I could see myself slipping and being impaled there like meat on a hook." William's hands clawed the air.

"Couldn't you crawl through it?"

"Uh-uh," he said. "No hope. It was a bramble bush of metal. No way.

"So I had to go under it. But the wire ran flat along the ground, stretched taut with hardly any give at all. I worked my way along the wall of wire looking for something that would give way just enough to let me through. And all the while I could see those two lights—the border post and the bus. And I knew my time was running out."

I glanced back to where the plum brandy was still passing from hand to hand. The fat Bulgarian official was staring—not at the bottle—but at the back of William's neck. I looked again and his eyes flicked from William to me and then back.

Then our train went under another tunnel and I put him out of my mind. Our passage echoed down the enclosing walls. The lights went out altogether.

"Guess they want us to sleep," said William.

"Not a chance." I lit a match and held it towards him. "Get your cigarette lit and get on with it."

He did.

"I didn't dare go closer to the border post," he said, "so I worked my way along the wire in the opposite direction, praying there wasn't a roving guard out there—or a land mine—or who knew what." The tip of his cigarette reddened and faded in several quick successions.

"I hit a post," he said. "A big, thick wooden post with wire wrapped around it from top to bottom. And just near the base, the ground sloped away a little to where I thought I had a chance. Just to be safe I shoved my pack under first. It was a tight fit, but no alarms went off and there it lay on the other side, waiting for me to come on through.

"So I lay down flat on my back and inched my face under the wire. Then my neck . . . my chest . . . and there I stuck. Stuck! The wire was caught on my jacket, but I couldn't get the jacket off. I couldn't go back. I couldn't go forward. I was just stuck. I took a deep breath and the wire bit into my chest. Stuck! For just a moment," William snickered, "for just a moment I lost it. Then I faced up to it. By exhaling as far as I could, my chest shrank down enough so it didn't hurt and I wormed forward as hard as I could. The wire shredded my coat, but I was moving, then I was under . . . I'd made it!

"When I rolled to my feet and grabbed my pack I was elated—absolutely elated—but I still had to be cautious. I started trotting towards the bus—on tiptoe, if you can imagine that. I wanted to cheer I was so happy . . . 100 yards to go . . . 50 . . . 30 . . . and then the bus started to move."

"What? I thought they were supposed to be waiting for you."

"The hour was up," said William. "That was the agreement. Not that that made me feel any better about it. What could I do? I started to run. The bus began to pick up speed and I was so desperate I had to risk yelling. 'Wait!' I shouted. 'Wait! Wait!'

"The bus stopped. I was almost there when there was a shout from the border post and I could hear boots pounding the pavement towards us. I put my hand on the door of the bus.

"The door opened and then FLASH—there were lights, search beams. We were in the spotlight just like that. Somebody fired shots into the air and I froze. The people in the bus were scrambling, yelling—"

"Why were the people in the bus so worried?"

"Contraband," he said. "The Englishman was bringing back a five kilo load of hash. He had it wrapped in tinfoil, sort of like a loaf of bread, and when the searchlights hit the bus, he knew what would happen. So the instant those lights flashed, he dug out that foil package and chucked it out the window.

"Then everybody shut up.

"I squinted my eyes against the light and put up my hands. The hook-nosed guy stepped out from behind the beams and slapped me across the face. In the darkness, the soldiers laughed. Then he gave an order, and three of them stepped onto the bus. All the passengers came out and stood in the road while the soldiers started stripping the interior, throwing out baggage and bottles, ripping at the seats.

"The hook-nosed man led the English driver and me back to his office. At first, he threatened to jail us both and impound the bus, but the Englishman gritted his teeth and wrangled back at him. I stayed quiet.

"Pretty soon you could see that what the Bulgarian wanted was a payoff. The Englishman breathed a little easier. I didn't, because I had nothing to pay with.

"Bargaining went on for quite awhile. Finally, one of the soldiers came in and spoke to the Bulgarian, who looked disappointed. They'd apparently found nothing. He dismissed the soldier.

"He sat and looked across at us for a minute, working his lips over his ugly mouth. Then he spoke to the Englishman.

'Damages,' he said. 'Forms. Much trouble here.' He waved a handful of papers at him and rubbed his thumb and forefinger together.

"The Englishman spoke up. 'Bus go,' he said, gesturing with his hand.

"Hook-nose nodded.

"The Englishman looked at me. I must have looked pretty miserable because he said to the official, 'He go?'

"The official shook his head. 'Visa,' he said.

"'No, no. He go back to Turkey. Get visa.'

"The official rubbed his fingers together again.

"The Englishman took out his wallet and threw down some pounds. 'For bus,' he said. He stopped and growled across at me. 'You bloody fool. I ought to let you waste away here.' Then he threw down some dollars and said, 'For him. Go Turkey.'

"The official's hand passed over the table and the money disappeared. The Englishman went out. Pretty soon I could hear the bus start up and the noise of the engine got fainter and fainter. Then it was gone.

"The official stood up and bared his rotting teeth. He leaned close 'til I could smell the staleness of his breath. He pointed a finger at the side of his head and said one word. 'Think.'

"'But he paid you,' I said.

"He gestured again. 'Think.'

"Then he went out of the room and locked the door."

"No honor among thieves, is there?" William's twitchiness began to appear ever more reasonable. The office of a certain inspector in Bucharest came to mind and I tried not to think of the list in my pocket.

William went on. "Whooo. You can bet I thought. Thought and stewed and bit my nails. Anything could happen and all of it bad. Time passed. Then more. I figured for sure that Hook-nose had decided just to pocket the money and keep me anyway. I was mad and scared and my intestines felt like they'd been used in a knot-tying competition. Things looked bad.

"Finally, Hook-nose came back in, lifted me out of my seat, and dragged me through the door. He pointed me again towards Turkey and kicked me hard in the seat of my pants.

"I took off. Nobody called after me."

I stared into the darkness while William sucked long and deep on the cigarette. The ember glowed, then faded. We sat in silence.

He sighed. "That's one night I'll never forget. And God help me if I ever have to do it again. There was no moon, hardly any stars. Just enough light to make the shadows move when you looked at them fast. You know that stretch of Turkey. Nothing out there. No traffic, nobody. Just sounds and shadows and sudden gusts of wind on your neck. I just walked.

"By morning I was exhausted—and I hadn't even made Edirne yet. But then I had a stroke of luck. A Turkish truck came steaming by and I danced and waved 'til my arms hurt. It stopped. The driver leaned out his window and yelled down at me. Just one word, but a lovely one. 'Istanbul?' he said.

"'Istanbul!' I yelled back.

"He was hauling manufactured goods back from Germany. Spoke a little German, in fact, so we got on all right. I told him a bit of my story and he sympathized. Even insisted I stay with him at his mother's house in Istanbul.

"I had him make one stop en route to his house: the Bulgarian Embassy. Then I slept 'til the following day. Friday morning I had my visa and Ahmed (my new friend) had put me on a train to Edirne at his expense.

"But I still had that border to face. And virtually no money. I didn't know if they'd let me cross, visa or no.

"I arrived mid-afternoon, so luckily the guards were different. Day shift, I figured. No Hook-nose and seemingly no one else that remembered me. My papers were in order, so in went the proper stamp and off I went.

"I walked a little way up the road and sat down on my pack to wait. I sure wasn't going to walk the length of Bulgaria, so I just had to hope for a lift from another trucker or somebody like that. But there was no traffic that day. I sat for an hour; for two. Nothing. It started to get cold and I was feeling worse and worse.

"I was sitting there staring when I noticed something glinting down in the gully off the side of the road. The angle of light was just right to pick it up.

"It took a moment, but then my brain clicked. I remembered the Englishman's package. I'd figured he'd picked it up before the bus left the border, but there must not have been a chance. I did a dance step alongside my pack. Five kilos of primo Afghani hash! My fortune was made. I took a step towards the gully and then stopped.

"I heard a motor in the distance. A truck—a big, international-type truck—was rolling out of customs. It might just be the last chance of the day. I couldn't decide; I teetered on the edge of the gully. The glint of light on the foil, the engine's rumble approaching . . . The truck stopped. Indecision, panic . . . I was right on the edge."

William's hand gripped mine in the darkness. "I had to have a ride. The night shift—and Hook-nose—might be coming on duty at any minute. Yet to leave the package, to waste such an incredible opportunity! I wavered. I cursed. I ran for the truck.

"I opened the passenger door and smiled in. 'Thank you, *merci, danke schoen,*' I said.

"The driver wagged his head.

"'One minute,' I said. I held up one finger and mimed the need to have a leak. The driver laughed and waved me off. I slid down into the gully and there it was. A tightly wrapped tin foil package. Five kilos! I laughed out loud. Five kilos! I tucked it under my coat and scrambled up the bank.

"The truck was there, idling. I got in and we started off in a great shifting and clattering of gears. I looked back out the rearview mirror. The border guards were being changed; the night shift had arrived."

❀ ❀

Our train went over a bump and the lights clicked back on. I looked across at William McGee. His forehead was shiny with sweat. He took a last drag on his cigarette and stubbed it out. His hand shook.

"You don't believe me, do you?" His head swiveled and his glasses stared at me. The light reflected so that his eyes were invisible. "You think I'm making it up."

"No . . ."

"Or at least exaggerating." He exhaled in a wheezing rush, and then dug under his seat and produced a faded canvas pack. His right hand disappeared inside. He fumbled, grunted, and then his hand reappeared. It held a largish foil package. "Sniff," he said, holding it up to my nose.

The smell was strong and sweet, and a little intoxicating even through the foil. There was no doubt as to the contents.

William put the package away and stuffed his gear back under the seat. I could find nothing to say. He felt in his pocket for another cigarette. "Damn, I'm out of smokes." He stood up. "I'll just try the dining car. Should get some there."

I turned and watched him go. He squeezed past the circle of brandy drinkers and through the door of the carriage. After a moment, the fat Bulgarian official wiped his mouth and stood up. He eased his bulk through the door behind him.

The lights went out again. The train rattled on. I fell asleep.

When I woke, pale slivers of morning sun slid through the window blinds. I massaged my aching neck. Two officials, a Yugoslav and an Austrian, came down the aisle and stopped at my seat. The Austrian border, I thought dimly.

"Passport," said the Yugoslav.

I fumbled it out.

They both eyed it briefly and handed it back. "Baggage." The Austrian spoke with Germanic precision. I indicated my bag. They prodded it in a desultory way, grunting in satisfaction.

"Yours?" The Austrian pointed at a dusty pack stuffed under the seat on my right. I remembered William McGee. Where in the world . . . ?

"No, no. Friend." I pointed back towards the dining car, praying my face would hide the growing fear and confusion I felt.

The Yugoslav reached under the seat and hauled out William's pack. I began to sweat. The officials patted around the outside and then the Austrian undid the top. He thrust in his hand.

I looked out the window. I couldn't bear to watch. Would I be held responsible? What were the penalties? I fought terror.

"Danke schoen."

I looked around in time to see the retreating back of both officials. William's pack lay resting on the seat beside me. I was stunned—they'd found nothing. Unable to resist, I dug down to where I'd seen William pull out the package. Nothing. I punched and prodded, shook and searched the pack inside and out. Nothing. The package was gone. So was William, I now realized, as the last vestiges of sleep finally seeped away.

I sat up straight, blinking sticky eyes. The coach was nearly empty. The drinkers near the door were gone, and in their stead a small man in a conductor's uniform busied himself with some papers.

I stood up a bit unsteadily and made my way back to the door. The conductor spoke up as I passed. "Toilet is other way," he said.

"Dining car," I said. "I'm just going to the dining car."

"Sorry," he said. "No dining car on this train."

No dining car. No William. No foil package. No fat Bulgarian official. I stood there in the aisle, rubbing my neck. My hand went to the list in my pocket. An empty bottle of plum brandy rolled noisily about beneath the seats. It was a Bulgarian brand.

# AT THE FOREST'S EDGE

❁ ❁ ❁ ❁

### 1977

FACES IN EVERY POLICE STATION; on every public building and post office wall. Newspaper stories, day after day. Snippets of conversations on the street, mutterings, and dark looks. "Baader-Meinhof," they said. Then people looked around them, worried that one of the gang—Ulrike Meinhof herself, perhaps—might be stalking the line of linden trees that fringed the boulevard.

Deaths and bombings. Random attacks. Politicians, financiers dragged from cars and shot. The Federal Republic had never seen anything like this. One had to go back further, to the Reich—and nobody, nobody at all, cared to exhume that.

There was no denying the Baader-Meinhof impact. Restaurants added armed security at their doorways. Police checks stopped cars on the outskirts of town. He'd felt the narrowed eyes, the heightened searches at the border posts, and knew he needed to move quietly. To sink down low.

❁ ❁

There was a trail leading down out of the forest. If followed north, it skirted the town, turning into a footpath that ran under the rim of the foothills, out of the valley, and into the hinterlands of High Bavaria.

But in the other direction, back into the forest, the trail ran up through the Gorge and south to the Austrian border. By day, with ice pillars and glints of a distant sky, the trail seemed almost picturesque. At night, the slippery rock surface turned hard and treacherous and nobody passed that way. Nobody except smugglers. But what would be worth smuggling between Germany and Austria? Something political, by all accounts. Perhaps to do with the American military and their recreation base just up the road.

It was cold in the forest. But when he came out from the line of trees, sunlight bounced off the snow pack and he shielded his eyes to see.

There was a lane in the distance, and beyond it a track that led over a hill and out of sight. The town would be on the other side, nestled into the river bend. Before he left the cover provided by the forest's edge, he scanned across the landscape—over dead stumps of field corn freckled with snow, past outlier birch trees mottled black and white like the sunnier patches of ground.

A plume of smoke rose along the horizon, opposite the direction of town. A farmstead, no doubt. Owner of these fields. There was always hope of a bed, or a rustic meal. Could he pass himself off as an itinerant laborer? A man of few—very few—words? Hard of hearing, or none too bright. Anything to disguise his smattering of Bayerisch Deutsch.

Maybe even a farmer's daughter . . .

But isolation bred observation. Better to hide in plain sight, in the town. Or might the border patrol be there prowling? Bored and looking for unfamiliar faces? Still . . . in town were more possibilities, and—if it came to it—more opportunities to run.

He needed to be in Partenkirchen by the 19th. If that meant Alpine walking, he would need fortification. All that was at hand was snow. He scooped up a handful and set off across the field, sucking reflectively at a snowball.

Ulrike would be waiting. She had to be.

# DUST TO DUST

❦ ❦ ❦ ❦

Herat, Afghanistan, 1974

Archibald Edwin Jones lay stretched out on a rope-strung bed in the last room on the left of the Minaret Hotel. He was a British subject, male, born in Leicester on 14 May 1953. He stood five foot six and weighed just over eight stone. This much could be told from the passport that lay open on the floor next to his left hand. His right hand gripped the dirty bit of sheet that half-covered his skinny body. The body was stiff.

The tall, thin American stepped across the packed dirt floor and bent to pick up the passport. Then he moved to the doorway, pushed aside the tattered length of curtain, and called into the courtyard. "Ashim," he said. "Ashim."

On the far side of the courtyard, a plump, turbaned form wiggled in the shade and sat up. The hotel manager, yawning from his heat-induced torpor, blinked across at the American.

"Ashim, come here."

The Afghan stirred himself and moved across the empty space. Puffs of dust trailed in his wake. The American waited, waving off the clusters of flies disturbed by his presence in the doorway. Ashim entered the room.

"A man is dead, Ashim."

"A man is dead?" The Afghan stared blankly at the body. He took a step closer, then retreated. "Man is dead?"

"Drug overdose, from the look of it."

"A man is dead. In my hotel." The Afghan's lips quivered. His face darkened. "In my hotel. Oh . . . oh!" He pushed through the curtain at the door and clapped his hands twice. "*Yekyeki!*" he called. "Yekyeki!"

A thick face appeared in a connecting doorway and Ashim shouted a series of commands. The face disappeared. Ashim looked back into the room. "Very bad for me. Police will come. Hotel close. Very bad." He began to moan. "Police, police. Very bad." He backed out of the doorway into the sun.

The American stood in the darkened room and flipped through the pages of the passport. Visas for Turkey and Iran, and a border stamp for Greece. He stopped at a firmly pressed official stamp that announced "*the bearer of this passport has been officially repatriated to the United Kingdom from the Grand Duchy of Luxembourg, 19 July 1973.*"

The broken chronicle of an interrupted life. Somewhere deep inside him, the American felt a slight, swimming surge of doubt.

The hotel manager reentered, wringing his hands. "Oh, my hotel. My family. Police will come to my family . . ." His hands gripped the American's arm. "Police are coming soon. You must leave this room."

"What's that?" The American looked up in distraction. "Oh right, the police. Right."

The Afghan departed, but the American looked again at the passport. It was the entry visa for Iran that bothered him. It was slightly smudged—and across from it was a very elaborate visa for the Cameroons that covered an entire page. Among other things, it took the trouble of stating that "*Archibald Edwoon shall not seek employment during his stay in Rupulbic of Cameroons.*" There were other misspellings as well.

"Here now, what're you doing in here?" A Cockney voice from the doorway interrupted the American's thoughts. A ferret-faced boy with a thin moustache moved into the room. "What've you got there? Give me that."

The American handed him the passport.

"That's Archie's. What's on here then?" He tried to look past to the beds.

The American blocked his view. "Your friend is dead," he said.

"What? You're lying." The Cockney shoved past him to the side of the bed. Then he stopped. His face went white and he began to shake. "What? What? What's this?"

The American took his arm and led him to the doorway. "Come on. Let's sit down outside and talk this over."

The boy looked back, his forehead pinched and furrowed against the white. "Archie," he said.

"Come on. Leave that here." The American tossed the passport back onto the floor and they went out the door.

❀ ❀

An awning that had once been a sandy brown covered a small portion of the dust-strewn courtyard. Flies buzzed in its shade, licking at the sticky remains of tea and yogurt on the lone table beneath the awning, where a handful of travelers sat staring at the sudden burst of activity in the hotel.

"*Ja.* I think they clean the rooms. That is most unusual." The speaker was German: a jut-jawed Teuton with a shaven head. "Never have I seen them clean the rooms."

The pale Frenchman on his left looked up and nodded. "*C'est vrai, ca. Pas normale.*" Long, stringy hair and beard all but obscured his face, giving him a look of experience that belied his age. He wore an Afghan shirt that hung past his knees and wide, billowing drawstring pants. "Pas normale." He wrapped a rag around the thick, cone-shaped chillum in his hands and lit it, puffing deeply, and then handed it to the auburn-haired woman seated beside him.

She drew on it twice and passed it on. "Not that it can be much of a cleaning. They've got nothing but cold water and a dirty rag."

Ashim came bustling past the awning.

The German hailed him. "Ashim, you clean the rooms, ja?"

"Yes, yes. Very busy, sorry."

He started on, but the German called after him. "The bugs. You must make all the bugs dead, Ashim."

The Afghan came back to where the travelers sat. His hands worked in agitation across his tunic. "Make bugs dead? A man is dead. Police will come." He shook a fat finger at the Frenchman. "Please you. No smoking of hashish when police are here. Big trouble for you. Big trouble for me." He nodded at his own wisdom and moved on towards the smoke-darkened room that served as the kitchen.

"*Qu'est qu'il a dit?* A man is dead?"

Two figures emerged from a doorway and approached the awning.

"Look," said the German. "The American."

The woman with the auburn hair stood up. "Peter's involved. What is this?"

There was a loud banging on the outer door of the courtyard. Ashim appeared and waddled towards the sound. He threw open the gates and four men in patched, discolored uniforms moved past him to stand in the courtyard. A cloud of dust blew in from the street outside and ran its way across the empty stretch of ground to the awning that flapped tiredly above the heads of the travelers. The Frenchman tapped out the chillum and put it away.

When the police emerged from the dead man's room they poked about in some of the adjacent quarters and then stalked over to the travelers still sitting in the only patch of shade. Peter and the dead man's roommate had joined the seated group.

The police halted just under the awning and shifted their ancient matchlock rifles into a rest position. The largest of them—a squint-faced man with a week's growth of beard and a hand-cut yellow badge pasted on his cap—spoke.

Ashim, hovering nearby, moved up to translate. "He say, who is dead man's friend?"

The Cockney lifted his head. "That's me."

"Please to see passport."

The Cockney hesitated.

Ashim's voice was smooth and well-oiled. "Please. You must give this."

The Englishman stood up, reached under his shirt, and handed his passport to Ashim. The manager passed it along to the policeman with the patch of yellow and pointed to the name. The policeman read aloud. "James Tyler Baker."

"Jimmy. That's me."

The policeman grunted out a rapid stream of words. Ashim looked at the ground. "James Tyler," he said. "You must go with this man." Then he looked up. "But not to worry. I will arrange everything."

"Arrange what? Why should I have to go with him?" The Cockney's voice wavered.

"I am so sorry. You are under arrest."

"Arrest!" Jimmy lurched backwards. "Arrest for what?"

The squint-faced policeman clapped his hands and two of the others moved up to stand on either side of the Englishman.

"Hang about! You can't just haul me off like that."

A rifle went down into his back and nestled there, tight against his shirt.

"Ashim!" said the Cockney, but Ashim only waggled his head and shrugged.

"Not to worry," he said. "I will fix."

The entourage marched to the outer door of the hotel compound with the Cockney still protesting and, beside him, Ashim patting his shoulder and muttering into his ear. They went out into the wind and behind them there was silence throughout the hotel.

❋ ❋

Just before noon there was another knock on the outer doors. The servant boy opened the doors and two policemen entered, followed by an elderly, white-bearded man in a ragged turban who carried an antique box camera over his shoulder. The policemen went into the room where the body lay, while the old man set down the enormous camera and began to assemble it.

The police came out of the room dragging the bed and the body between them into the midday heat. At the outer wall of the compound they stopped and attempted to prop the death bed up. The body slipped off. They tried again, but the bed fell sideways. On the third attempt they succeeded, wedging it at an awkward angle against the wall.

The old photographer adjusted his piled turban and put his head under the black curtain at the rear of the camera. One hand held a black rubber bulb, and when he pressed it, a small poof of powder exploded from the camera. His head reappeared, turban askew, and he fiddled with the mechanisms. Then he repeated the process. After the second picture, the photographer and the policemen moved into the shade of an adjacent room. The camera and the body remained in the white heat of the courtyard.

The travelers watched from under the awning with increasing distaste and diminishing curiosity. When the servant boy poked his head out from the kitchen, Peter called over to him. "Yekyeki. The sun is too hot. It is bad for the body. Tell them to move it." He gestured towards the body.

The boy stared slack-jawed for a moment and then stepped out of the kitchen, wiping crumbs from his mouth and trailing a dirty bit of rag behind him like a pet. He called across the courtyard and the old man stepped into the sun. He crossed over to the camera, picked it up, and carried it carefully back into the shaded room.

The sun beat down from overhead and now the body on the bed cast no shadow. The heat was intense and debilitating. The travelers looked away.

"Peter, you must do something." The auburn-haired woman looked miserable. "It's making me ill," she said. "It's not right."

The tall American studied his sandals. "There's nothing I can do, Margaret. They wouldn't understand. If only Ashim were back . . ."

The bald German spoke up. "He is making free the English, I think. Maybe he comes soon."

As the sun inched across the sky the body began to bloat. Still it lay propped on the bed against the wall of the courtyard; the face growing puffy and purple splotches appearing on the cheeks. Flies settled thick in the hair. The smell of heat and death lay heavy on the windless air.

After a bit, Archibald Edwin Jones began to slide slowly down the length of the bed and the sheet slipped off his body. Flies swarmed.

Margaret went to her room.

There were dark circles under Jimmy's eyes. His face was pale and his hands shook when he tried to light a cigarette. "It was me dreams," he said, puffing furiously at the ill-lit cigarette. "Dreams, nightmares, whatever the hell they were. I mean to say, Archie going down was bad enough, but staring a stretch in an Afghan prison in the face . . ." He broke off and shuddered.

"But surely you're off the hook now," said Peter. "Ashim got you out of jail, didn't he?"

"Oh, aye. Ashim was great stuff at the station. But it's by no means settled that I'm free. I've still got this lot with me." He jerked his head backwards towards the door of the kitchen, where a flat-headed soldier with a leathery face squatted on his heels against the mud wall of the cooking area, stuffing chunks of bread into his mouth. One leg of his pants rode high above the other and his shoes were worn with the heels trod down. A matchlock rifle stood propped at his side.

"Quite," said Margaret.

"Goes everywhere with me, he does," said Jimmy. "Even sleeps in me room at night. Maybe he give me the dreams."

"You are having dreams?" The German moved under the awning and sat next to Jimmy.

"Dreams? Oh, let me tell you about dreams. Drove me bloody mad last night—"

"Ja, I too have had dreams. One year I was in India, I dream every night I am out of my body. I am leaving my body and passing upwards through the ceiling . . ." The German jutted his jaw and lifted his arms skyward, enmeshed in his own concerns.

The Cockney stubbed out his cigarette and lit another. His moustache twitched with nerves.

Margaret clapped her hands until the servant boy appeared, and ordered a pot of tea. When it arrived, Ashim accompanied it.

"My friend, my friend, how you are today?" He bent over the Cockney, straightening unnecessarily at the back of the boy's chair.

"Sit down, Ashim. Join us." Peter pulled up a chair. "Tell me, why would the police be making an arrest? Can't they see that the boy just took too many drugs?"

Ashim put his hand to his forehead and shook his head. "Before last year, maybe no problem. But now, king is gone. Finish." He brushed his hands together as if cleaning them of crumbs. "Now, it is friends of Russians who make these rules. Always so many rules." The Afghan looked suddenly tired and he muttered a line in Farsi. "We have proverb," he said. "'When milk is spilled, the dogs will eat.' This Archibald make many problems for us."

"Archie's dead. You leave off him." The Cockney's face flushed with anger.

"Please my friend. Listen one moment. First problem is this—boy died from drugs. This police know. But what drugs? In Afghanistan we have hashish, opium, yes, like that. But this boy has take something other."

"Heroin?"

"I don't know, but this is coming from Iran. First problem then is a smuggling. Police are look at passport of Archibald. They look at passport of James Tyler. Both go Iran together. They think, maybe both smuggle. They look something funny with passport."

Peter looked across at Jimmy, but the Cockney was staring at the ground. His bony hands rubbed slowly up and down the length of his trousers.

Ashim went on. "Second problem, this. These boys come in Afghanistan only one day. To come in Afghanistan, they must show money. Paper of Archibald say '*I have one hundred fifty dollar.*' Paper of James Tyler say '*I have three hundred fifty dollar.*' Now Archibald dead. Police find no money. They look in this man pocket, find five hundred dollar. They think this man kill Archibald to take money."

"That's crazy. That's a lie!" Jimmy jumped to his feet and almost upset the tea table. "I wouldn't kill me mate for a hundred and fifty quid, let alone dollars. That's crazy."

"Sit down, Jimmy. We know that."

"Archie didn't have no money. He never had no money. What he had run out in Istanbul. I told him I'd stake him as far as Kabul. Then when we get to the border we suddenly got to show some cash. Hundred fifty minimum. I slipped him some of mine. Now they think I killed him for me own money. It's daft, I tell you. Daft."

"So. He goes then to Kabul with no money." The German's bullet head swiveled. "Then what?"

"He reckoned we'd just go to the Embassy and get sent home. Piece of cake, he said. Done it before, no problem."

Peter poured himself some more tea and stirred absently. He was thinking of passport entries. There was the repatriation stamp from Luxembourg . . . and that elaborate visa from the Cameroons. "When was Archie in Africa?"

"Africa? He was never in Africa."

"Was he planning to go?"

The Cockney looked puzzled. "Not him."

"Oh, my mistake. I thought somebody told me you were going to Cameroons together."

"Cameroons? Oh . . . well . . . that never worked out, did it?" Jimmy stuck a cigarette in his mouth and tried to light a match. His hands shook badly. After three attempts he gave up, threw down the cigarette, and swore. "Blimey, I wish I were gone from here. Ashim, you don't reckon they'd actually do me?"

The Afghan offered a quick, sleek smile. "No no, my friend. I will arrange everything. Is very bad for my family."

"Prison here—I have heard such stories." The German's jaw jutted even further as he clamped his teeth together.

Ashim stared into the distance. "Is very bad. Very bad." He rubbed his forehead, leaving a dark smear above his eye.

"I have heard that they beat here the prisoners," prodded the German.

"Oh, they beat, they beat. Every day. They have very long thing like rope, with nine ends. Very bad. Only food is coming one *chapati* and a little water."

"And the cells?"

"Cells?"

"The rooms," said the German.

"Hah hah." Ashim's laugh lay dead on his lips. "No room. You just live in hole in ground. Above you is man with beating thing." Again he rubbed at his face. Then he looked back at the Cockney. "Come, my friend. We go again to police. Finish business."

The two of them stood up. The soldier against the wall stood too and Jimmy took a slow, stumbling step out from the awning. The doors rattled as they opened and the gusting wind blew sandy pillars of dust inward across the empty courtyard. The gates banged shut. Again the stillness and the heat settled over the Minaret Hotel.

❈ ❈

The Frenchman boarded the bus at the edge of a row of shops. The bazaar was emptying rapidly as the sun approached its zenith. A few women covered from head to foot in tent-like robes still squatted over limp vegetables and dusty, faded bolts of cloth. Then, one by one, they abandoned bartering and retreated in slow-moving clusters to their home compounds. The traders loosened their turbans, lay back deep in the shade of their tiny stands and fanned themselves to sleep.

The Frenchman shuffled barefoot onto the bus and picked his way through the garbage and the grain sacks that clogged the aisle between the slatted benches. A window seat was empty, and the Frenchman took it. He wiped at the dusty glass with his sleeve and stared through it at the street of shops.

Out in the sun, four men in mismatched uniforms struggled with a very large wooden crate, rectangular in shape and at least the length of a man. They fought it up and onto the roof of an aging Ford whose driver sat behind the wheel and periodically spat gobs of green onto the ground outside the car.

Once the crate was lashed onto the top, the driver came to life. He leaned out his window and bellowed to the bazaar at large, "Kandahar, Kabul. Kandahar, Kabul." He inched the car down the rutted street between the shops. "Kandahar, Kabul." A young boy ran out from a shop and flagged him down.

Two female figures enveloped in vermillion cloth hobbled out to the waiting car where they jabbered briefly with the driver. Then one of them backed away and pointed at the crate on top. The driver made a vague gesture with his head. An unseen hand touched a veiled nose. The women backed away. The driver shrugged and rolled on. "Kabul, Kandahar," he called.

The wind gusted and shifted, blowing from the car past the Frenchman's bus window. He held his breath 'til it passed, but the odor lingered on the air. Dust settled on his teeth, leaving the taste of grit and a sense of mortal decay.

The car reached the end of the street, still without passengers. "Kabul, Kandahar," called the driver.

❈ ❈

They would take the Englishman aside and reprimand him, Peter told himself. Then Ashim would make the pay-offs and the whole affair would be dismissed. There was no reason to worry.

He stood on top of the back wall of the Minaret Hotel, looking off over the rock-strewn foreground speckled with huts and layered dung-cakes set aside for fuel. A naked boy chased a goat around a tiny courtyard and a thin trail of smoke rose from one of the further huts. Beyond the huts, a graveyard wound back into the hills: whitewashed tombs pulverizing slowly into dust and baking in the heat of the desert sun.

Margaret had wanted him to intercede . . . to demand . . . to do something. That wasn't the way of the East, he'd said. One had to learn to just wait. The smudged passport and the needless entry visa for the Cameroons still played in the back of his mind, but that was by the by; of no interest to the police.

Off in the distance behind him, the low murmur of town life continued. In the dim, cool interiors of mosques, old men prayed and dreamed. Somewhere a *tonga* passed, its whipcrack sharp against the sound of clopping hooves. Above the town, the thick-walled fortress built by Alexander the Great still stood as a sign to the nomad caravans that roamed the empty mountains of the country's interior. The fortress—and four ancient minarets set out like chess pieces over the patchwork squares of desert shadow—marked the effective limit of Afghanistan. Beyond that, the dust and the sun were king.

Peter thought again of Ashim's prison holes and then set the image aside. It was time to move on. Time to cross the brown expanse of Afghan hills and take Margaret out of the desert grit and down the Khyber to the lush green lowlands of the Indian subcontinent. The Englishman would be all right.

He looked once more over the sepia tones of the drowsing city and wondered what the nomads felt. Somewhere in the distant brown haze was a huddle of huts that claimed to mark the border—and across a stretch of no-man's-land, another huddle that bore the flag of Iran. But all that was so much make-believe.

It was the moon that ruled by night . . . and the sun, the merciless sun, that ruled by day.

Even nomads paid obeisance to the sun. Peter climbed down from the compound wall. The dust and heat lay heavy on the town.

❦ ❦

Weeks later, Peter and Margaret sat eating yogurt beneath the ceiling fan of a dingy restaurant in the capital of Pakistan. The door opened, a man entered, and a moment later a voice ordered tea in a familiar French accent.

Margaret looked up. Her hand touched his. "Look, Peter, it's that Frenchman. The one from the Minaret Hotel."

Peter shifted his body for a better view. "So it is." He called across to the other table. "Hello, *Monsieur du Minaret*."

The Frenchman looked round, peering through his matted length of hair. Then his eyes lit up in recognition. "Ah, *mes amis*." He came across to their table and sat. "Peter, yes? And Margaret."

"That's us," said Margaret, and she smiled. "Welcome to Pindi."

The Frenchman snorted. "Pah. Was much better Afghanistan. You have seen Bamiyan Valley?"

Peter whistled through his teeth. "The Buddhas? Incredible." All three smiled at the memory.

An old man shuffled up, rattling a cup of tea and placed it at the Frenchman's side. He sipped at the steaming liquid.

"Did you ever see the Englishman again?" Peter asked. "The one who was arrested for murder."

"*Moi? Non, non.*" The Frenchman wiped at his scraggly beard. "I leave before you, *n'est pas*? Ah, but I see the . . . the box for dead." His arms gestured in description.

"The coffin, you mean? For the dead boy?"

"*Oui, oui.* I go on bus to Kabul same day as box."

"It went on one of those buses?" Margaret was shocked.

"Non. No. In taxi. But bus go on same road, non? Before bus come to Kandahar we go pass this taxi. It was stop in desert. Broken." The Frenchman gulped at his tea. "Was nothing. Nothing there. Only sun . . . and nomads." He laughed in spite of himself. "Just taxi man and many nomad people with camels. They look this strange thing."

"And the bus stopped?" Margaret nodded expectantly across the table.

"*Naturellement.* Is nothing there. We take with us taxi man. Oh, yes."

"But what about the other passengers in the taxi? Surely it was packed to the running boards. And the coffin—what about it?"

The Frenchman shrugged. "Coffin stay in desert with the nomads. What else? Was no passengers." He finished his tea and stood up. "I go now to smoke." At the door he paused. "And the English boy. This Jimmy. What happen him?"

Peter looked down at his sandals. Margaret's hand was stroking through her auburn braids and she looked out the doorway past the Frenchman. "They put him in a taxi for Kabul," she said. "The coffin was on top."

For a long moment the Frenchman stood silent in the doorway. Then he turned and went out. Margaret watched him cross the street, hunching against the dust that blew across his path.

Her hand reached out for Peter's.

# UNTO US, THE SPOILS

❦ ❦ ❦ ❦

IN A BACK ALLEY WALK-UP in central Bombay, Radhakrishnan Gopti laid out a freshly pressed European shirt on the rope-strung cot that served as bed, sitting room, and nerve center for his entrepreneurial endeavors. Anand, the *dhobi-wallah*, had scorched a small section of the bottom of the shirt, and for a moment young Mr. Gopti considered refusing to make payment.

But the complications of finding another dhobi-wallah—one who never questioned whisky stains and lived close enough for discreet daily delivery—seemed incommensurate with the damage done. Instead, Mr. Gopti tucked the white shirt carefully into the top of his trousers until the scorch mark disappeared and then added a light dusting of talcum powder to his neck where the collar rode tight. He regretted the lack of a belt—appearances were crucial in his line of work—but felt, at least, that the tucking in of his shirt more closely simulated European dress.

The talc, of course, was a deliberate mark of sensitive respectability, though Mr. Gopti doubted at times whether this was evident to the foreign mind. He closed the door to his room, smoothed once at his oiled hair, and began to walk down the rickety stairs to street level. Perhaps today would be a productive one.

At the airport customs desk, a droopy-eyed official in khaki poked with his foot at the heaped baggage piled on the cement floor. Behind him, three men in identical uniforms slept peacefully atop their desks, legs curled up beneath their chins. The fattest one was snoring. The line of transit passengers stretched back towards the arrival gates, but the official showed no sign of haste. He fanned himself with a sheaf of currency declaration forms and yawned. Bombay in March was hot, and getting hotter. Even in the dissipating darkness of false dawn the heat hung like a blanket across the interior of the airport concourse.

Raymond Jax stood on the other side of the desk, wearing a limp wash-and-wear "embassy shirt," two hollow-heeled shoes, and an expression of mixed boredom and respect. Tiny rolls of undeclared dollars pressed against the belt lining of his pants, but he resisted the urge to scratch. Behind him, his partner Adriana had withdrawn into a private interior dreamspace that would be broken only when they passed on to the other side of the desk. It was her defense against any and all guises of bureaucracy and Raymond often envied her detachment.

The customs official, with another yawn, picked up the two American passports and flipped idly through their pages. "From where you are coming?" he asked, and at Raymond's response of "Kenya," he allowed one eyebrow to rise and then fall. "What is your purpose in India?"

Raymond answered as he always did. "Tourist."

The official's eyes slid up from where they had focused on a handwritten form. "You are declaring six hundred dollars travelers' cheques only, and the woman two. No cash. You are having return ticket?"

"We're going back to the States from here," said Raymond. "There's money being wired to us."

"Wired?" said the official, and a long conversation ensued regarding the advisability of such a measure and the unfortunate regulations, which nonetheless insisted upon proof of solvency at point of entry.

Raymond was prepared for all this. He would never have dreamt of waiting for money to be wired to an Indian bank (the length and frustration of such waits were a frequent source of amusement in travelers' watering holes), but his financial circumstances could not bear official scrutiny. Raymond put on a face of diligent respect, waggled his head in synchrony with the droopy-eyed official, and quietly set two packets of 555 cigarettes on the edge of the customs desk as he gestured once more for understanding and the return of the two passports.

Later, as the Americans picked past the porters in frayed colonial-era jackets and the splintering band of once-fellow passengers, Adriana said, "Just once I'd like to actually have some money waiting for us."

"Soon as I offload the duty-free stuff we'll be all right for a couple days."

"I mean for more than a couple days. That cash you've got tucked away will barely cover the plane tickets home and there's no way we're spending any part of that."

"There's always the checks," said Raymond.

"The checks! Those things might do for a customs form, but any bank will look up the numbers."

Raymond shifted his bag as they reached the outer doors. "They were dumped in Egypt. Those numbers won't be on anybody's system. Not yet."

"No, the camera guy *told* you they were reported in Egypt. Personally, I think he'd made them up in the back of his shop with one of his special box cameras."

"We'll get something cooking."

"I mean it. There's no English teaching jobs on the market *here*, and I'll be damned if I'm going to do day labor."

❀❀

Radhakrishnan Gopti had made three circuits of the promenade along the Gateway of India, with nothing to show for his troubles but a drenched right leg where some fool of a fisherman had tossed his catch without properly noting Mr. Gopti's impending intersection.

He sat down after this, on a bench at an outdoor tea stand, and ordered a small cup of tea and a sticky bun, calculating the cost against his profit margin. Perhaps if he tried the central train station . . .

At the airport, three Europeans with plastic briefcases and Soviet haircuts had commandeered the last taxi. Raymond was muttering—not at the prospect of taking a bus—but at the taxi driver's disinterest in his plastic bag of Johnny Walker Red and the partially opened carton of 555's. The sun was just peeking above the horizon line and already the back of his shirt was wet with sweat. He and Adriana moved slowly towards the bus stand.

For less than a rupee the No. 17 city bus carried passengers from the airport down past dusty fields and cement factories; along collections of wattled cardboard huts, crumbled temples, and sleeping strings of people and cows. Entire villages seemed to live in the wastelands beyond the roadway verge: small, dark men in ragged undershirts lay motionless across rope beds; scraps of paper, bits of metal, drying patties of dung lay heaped around them. Even at dawn, the air was thick with floating particles and portents of the waiting heat.

On the open-air upper deck of the bus, Adriana put her head on her arms against the back of the seat in front of her and watched the roadside struggle awake. Old men tottered into the fields to squat, eyes blank as they relieved themselves. Naked children pissed where they stood, staring into the rising edge of sun. Mothers, worn and thin as bundles of straw, fanned the coals of last night's fire and offered their breasts to babies. Children rolled up the strips of straw and cardboard they used as bedding; whole families stepped out of houses made of cardboard and scrap metals and gathered around the dung fires whose smoke hazed the fields behind them. Orange smoke floated along the horizon.

Adriana was a seasoned traveler, a veteran of the Indian roads from a visit five years before, but after the cool green highlands of Kenya, the road into Bombay seemed a vision of death. Some day, she thought, she'd get Raymond to retire to a Greek island. Or give up his constant scheming and find a legitimate source of income. Some day, maybe soon, she wouldn't be able to do this any longer. The suffering was too real.

Buildings multiplied. The city swallowed the road.

Then, as the bus honked its way through the narrowing street corridors, it passed a low-caste quarter of unpainted slab buildings and open sewers. Cows nosed about in search of food. The inhabitants sat cross-legged against the walls of their tenements— unpainted, unremarkable—and knit garlands of flowers: yellow, ochre, saffron. Their work piled up around them in heaps and mounds. Small mountains of marigolds spilled over the sidewalk. The scent overpowered even the filth of sewage. There, amidst grey-brown dinginess (almost an inversion of color, a drabness so blank as to be invisible), the brightness of the flowers was like a stab of paradise and Adriana saw that what she had been watching was not a vision of death, but a triumph won daily: the triumph of life in the midst of death. Would she ever have the strength for that?

The bus set the travelers down at the stone memorial arch on the edge of the port: the Gateway of India, which marked out the trading depot chosen by the British for glory. A quick glimpse of the archway was all they got, for the hawkers were swift and merciless.

"*Sar,* sar, you want guide, sar? Number one." A weedy man with a thin moustache and oversized bellbottoms pulled at Raymond's sleeve. Two pint-sized peanut vendors attached themselves to Adriana, circling her skirts and offering up handfuls of nuts and shells with a clamor of squeaking voices. A rickshaw driver hooted for attention from the curb, and at the sea's edge a cluster of peddlers gathered up their wares and scuttled towards the growing maelstrom.

The travelers dodged, running first obliquely away from the sea and then, as the looming glass-and-steel of Bombay's finest hotel—the Taj Mahal—intervened, back again towards the flagstone promenade and the tattered sheet that served as shade for a curbside tea stand.

Mr. Gopti had been nursing his tea for over half an hour when a sudden flurry of street vendors emitted two European figures who ran a zigzag course along the sea front and then slid to a halt under the shaded canopy above the tea stand. As the pack of vendors descended, Mr. Gopti waved them off, claiming that the foreigners were old friends of his and the possessors of a rare and deadly disease.

When the last of the street vendors had slunk away (the weedy man with the moustache, who tossed up a final "You want guide, sar?" before departing), the Europeans tipped their glasses to Mr. Gopti. "Thanks for saving us, whatever it was you said."

"No problem, my friends." Mr. Gopti smoothed his hand back over his pomaded hair. "I am emissary of my country." He knew enough to go no further.

The Europeans had gulped down their first cups of tea and were halfway through their second when the woman called over the proprietor of the tea stand and asked if he knew of a hotel nearby.

"Cheap," added the man beside her.

The proprietor pointed across the street. "My brother is having hotel just here you see." A bleached-out sign in Marathi script was tacked above a peeling doorway.

❦ ❦

They crossed the street to the hotel, and as they entered the doorway, Raymond narrowly avoided hitting a red-faced Sikh who was sputtering into his rolled-up beard. The Sikh adjusted his turban and curled his lip in their direction. "Personally, I prefer air," he said, and pushed past them into the street.

The Sikh, they quickly saw, had a point. The rooms were small and windowless. There was a shower and toilet down the hall—though it was difficult to tell which was which. The ceiling fan rattled painfully with every revolution, though this noise was all but drowned out by the shrill Indian film music blaring from a nearby room. The price, at least, was something they could afford.

"Maybe just for the night," said Raymond.

Adriana, who'd been through all this with Raymond too many times before, massaged her shoulder, shrugged, and said at last, "At least it isn't Lahore."

They set down their bags.

Raymond flopped onto the bed, pulled off his shoes, and replaced them with flip-flops. Adriana nudged her toe against the hollow heel of Raymond's discarded shoe. "I thought those things were going to keep us out of places like this."

"If the border hadn't been closed—"

"If the border hadn't been closed there would have been some other problem. There always is."

"Don't start that." Raymond lay back on the bed and covered his face with his arm. "The diamond deal only works if you go straight to the mines. The army has everything else wrapped up."

"You always have an answer, don't you?" Adriana slammed the door and moved reluctantly down the hallway towards the toilet. "One of these days—" And then she was singing to herself, "—One of these days a change is going to come."

Within twenty minutes, they'd laid out their things, learned that the water in the shower was off until dawn, and grown sufficiently tired of the film music that they decided to sate themselves with tea.

"I'm going to flog the whisky," said Raymond. "And then see if I can change money."

"You're not seriously going to try those checks at a bank?"

Raymond looked indignant. "Of course not. But they'll do for the street."

Outside, the heat seemed to grow stronger with every passing minute.

At the tea stall, Mr. Gopti watched the Europeans cross the road and resettle themselves nearby. They seemed to be arguing, or at least the woman looked perturbed. Sometimes that was a problem, but their discord might also prove useful. Mr. Gopti swirled the dregs of his cup and drank it off. When the Europeans had refilled their cups he stood up, smoothed once at his hair, and bowed slightly as he passed their bench.

"Good day to you, my friends," he said. "Should you require any assistance, please only to ask. I am at your service."

"Well, actually . . ." The man rattled a plastic bag between his legs and opened it far enough for Mr. Gopti to see the label on the bottle inside.

Half an hour later, transaction completed, Mr. Gopti was enthusiastically leading his new friends in the direction of a nearby, but little-known, Parsi fire temple. Their route took them through a backstreet market with merchants hawking grains, fruit, vegetables, plastic dishes, lanterns, and assorted pots and pans. The merchants loaded up handheld scales with rice or coconuts and calculated on their fingers. At one stall, while the woman hovered over scents and insisted the man offer his opinion, Mr. Gopti made a quiet purchase of almond-colored powder done up in a tiny square of cloth.

When they emerged from the market, Mr. Gopti, judging the moment right, drew them back from the sidewalk bustle and took the plunge. "Excuse me, sar," he began, wagging his head lightly from side to side. "I know you are busy man. But I can make very generous offer for you." He gestured with his hand open, twirling his fingers tight into his palm so that only thumb and forefinger remained outstretched, pointedly emphasizing his words. "I am businessman you see. I wish to go to London for seeing my brother. But government is making new law—fifty per cent taxation on foreign currency. Very bad."

The man shook his head in sympathy, or so it seemed to Mr. Gopti. "They've got the same deal in Kenya. Half the Asian businesses are folding and the rest are being forced to sell out."

Mr. Gopti brightened. "You are understand then?"

"I know how it works in East Africa. I don't remember seeing it in India, though. Bet there's a hell of a black market."

"Indeed, sar," said Mr. Gopti, drawing them further into the narrow shadow along a building wall. "Please to allow me to explain one minute. I have dollars. But I cannot go in bank to buy traveler cheques. Bank will charge this fifty per cent. However, sar, if you go in bank they will not charge you." He placed the tip of his forefinger gently on the man's chest.

The man studied the finger. "Why would I do that?"

"Suppose . . ." Mr. Gopti drew the word out. "Suppose I give you dollars, you buy cheques, then sign cheques over to me." He paused, beaming. "For this, I pay you twenty per cent. Very good commission for you."

❈ ❈

To Raymond, this pitch bore all the traces of a successful deal he'd negotiated on the shores of Lake Victoria the previous fall. "So you give me, say, a hundred dollars . . ."

"No, no sar. Thousand dollars. Maybe more."

"You give me a thousand dollars. I walk in and buy checks, come out and sign them over to you and you give me two hundred dollars cash? Is that right?"

"That is correct. Twenty per cent cost is better than fifty per cent cost. Yes?"

Raymond looked at Adriana and calculated. Two hundred dollars in India, at the rate they operated on, was a month's living for two. Anything that could buy time . . . He'd done transactions for duty-free goods, for re-dated plane tickets, for dumped and stolen travelers' checks, and once even a complicated three-way exchange of four different currencies that had netted him fifty dollars more than had been expected. This one looked eminently doable, though by the look on Adriana's face, she was just barely tolerating it.

Next to them on the wall was a poster of Ganesh, the plump elephant god, which drew worshippers with incense sticks and handfuls of produce. Adriana, looking increasingly impatient, was being buffeted by a steady stream of passersby.

The Indian interceded. "Please. Here it is very hard to think. Too much people and noise. Please. You come with me. We go to Royal Hotel, very quiet." He laid his hand on Adriana's arm. "On Marine Drive. I am meeting another couple there, Australian. They too are changing money for me. We have breakfast and talk in peace. Okay?"

Raymond was already calculating. At worst it was a free breakfast. And if the guy had other people already lined up, then this thing must run pretty smoothly. Adriana shook her head once and then shrugged. The Indian stopped a taxi. They all hopped in.

The Royal Hotel was very quiet. And very plush. Adriana

found herself, almost against her will, liking it on the spot. A short, smiling man in a white turban opened the door and, once inside, the noises of the street receded into the distance. Their new friend marched them past the desk and into the restaurant, where they occupied a table by the window looking across Marine Drive to the eastern shores of the Indian Ocean.

Directly outside the hotel, the road paralleled the shore and waves splashed over the verge. A little further along, a beach began, widening as it receded away. She could see groups of people moving here and there along the shore—women in bright, swirling saris; some Sikhs—or perhaps Rajputs, it was difficult to tell at this distance—but she could hear nothing.

"You like?" said the Indian.

She nodded and watched a boy with a kite run against the wind.

"Is Chowpatty Beach," he said. "Very famous beach. Maybe you know?"

"Why is it famous?" she asked, but already his attention had moved on.

A waiter appeared. The Indian gave a swift order and the waiter withdrew.

Their friend fingered his collar. "Ah, but I forget," he said. "Now we are settled, introductions are in order. I am Radhakrishnan. But you can call me Roddy."

Adriana was staring out the window. She knew the form—she wasn't expected to answer. It would be all Raymond and the Indian.

"I'm Raymond."

"Ray? Like sun ray, yes?"

"Raymond."

"Okay. Ray man."

Roddy looked very pleased and launched into a long explanation of governmental regulations, his family carpet business (which necessitated regular currency exchanges), and various Indian cultural matters. He was a nice chap, obviously at ease in the Royal, and just as obviously had a money problem that could be solved to their mutual advantage.

It was East Africa all over again. Idi Amin and his ouster of all resident Asians, obtuse government regulations, graft, and distrust . . . She and Raymond hadn't set foot in a bank for months. Indian merchants in Africa led a perpetual search for foreign currency as a hedge against sudden departure, and Raymond had used this fact to develop any number of profitable contacts. She hoped that Raymond wouldn't exploit the situation here overmuch, though she could scarcely complain if he did.

That was the problem. She was too acquiescent to Raymond's force of personality. Too dependent on his whims and decisions. Here he was, playing this little man along like a mouse fiddling with a prime bit of cheese. She wouldn't be surprised if he was angling to offload those dodgy checks onto the poor fellow.

Sometimes she wondered why she ever stayed with him at all.

They ran through the procedure once again, and then as the waiter at last reappeared, bearing—to Raymond's slight disappointment—only a pot of tea, Roddy paused. "There is one problem I have, however." He frowned slightly. "One time I am give one Frenchman dollars to buy cheques. When he comes out of bank he will not sign them to me. He shouts and such and says these are *his* cheques." Roddy looked down. "What I can do? Later, I find out this Frenchman has no money of his own. He was like . . . thief." He waggled his head sadly. "So now I ask, if you want me give you thousand dollars, first you show me you have thousand dollars. Just show," he added. "Then I know you are not man without money."

Raymond was figuring . . . if they included the cash for the flight home . . . between that and the dumped checks, showing a thousand was no problem. More immediately, his stomach was rumbling. "And breakfast? When's that coming?"

"Oh, soon, soon." Roddy waved his hand. "We are just waiting for Australian couple to join us."

While they waited and sipped at their tea, Roddy admired Adriana's bangles and recommended a good goldsmith in the Parsi quarter. To Raymond's disgust, she actually seemed to want to follow up the tip.

Then the door opened and in walked an Australian—tall, reddish-haired, with a walrus moustache and faded blue eyes. He greeted Roddy, who asked, "Your wife? Where is she today?"

"Oh, she felt like shopping," said the Aussie. "I mean, we did all this bit yesterday. It's only me that's got to go to the bank." He looked towards Raymond and winked. "Back for more," he said. "Let me little lady spend part of the profit."

"This is Jacko," said Roddy and began to re-explain everything for the Aussie, who waved him off.

"I know the drill. Let's just get on with it."

That sounded good to Raymond, despite the fact that breakfast had still not arrived and he was getting weak from lack of sustenance. In fact, his head was beginning to hurt more by the minute. "Here, let me show you my money." He began digging for his valuables pouch.

"No, no, no." Roddy stopped him. "It is not me you must show, but my uncle. He has the dollars. We go now to see him. He works in bank. I will call."

Roddy got up and headed out for the phone. The Aussie let loose a smile that ran up the left side of his mouth. "Good scam this, eh?"

"Well, we haven't actually done it yet," Adriana replied.

He looked surprised. "Oh no? Hah—we ran through it yesterday. Worked a charm." He leaned back and twirled his moustache. "Reckon I'll keep it up as long as Roddy'll have me." He cocked an eye towards Raymond. "Say though, show him as much as possible. You can make more."

"How's that?"

"Well I mean . . . if you've got fifteen hundred, say, of your own to show, then his uncle will hand over fifteen hundred cash. At twenty per cent, that's an extra hundred right there."

"This uncle . . ." Raymond began.

Jacko waved his hand. "Don't mind him. Suspicious old bird, that's all. Thinks we're all about to run off with the dough."

"I guess some people do," put in Adriana.

The Aussie shrugged. "Yeah, well . . ."

Roddy reappeared. "Very good then. All set?"

No mention of breakfast. For a moment, Raymond considered complaining. But then, what did it matter? In an hour or so they'd have enough money to buy a hundred breakfasts. He fought off the growing headache as he stood up.

Everybody went back out on the street. Outside the air-conditioned hotel the air was thick and the heat came on in waves. Mr. Gopti dabbed at his neck with a handkerchief. Across from him, the man seemed almost to stagger for a moment. Mr. Gopti noticed the woman leaning weakly against a lamppost.

"You are alright, madam?" he inquired. She nodded and wiped a hand across her forehead. He wagged a finger sideways. "Better you rest." He hailed a cab and then turned to Raymond, his brow furrowed with concern. "Better your wife wait for us at Taj Mahal Hotel. I am thinking she is tired."

While the man considered this, weaving slightly himself, Mr. Gopti slipped the driver a bill with the words "Taj Mahal," and Adriana was bundled into the back seat of the cab.

Mr. Gopti hovered as the man Raymond leaned in and spoke. "There's really no point in you dragging around with us."

The woman nodded, still a touch pale. "I'm just not feeling well at the moment."

"It is natural, madam. Heat is very awful this time of year."

The man looked back at him in annoyance, but Roddy ploughed on.

"Better you come after monsoon. Sky is clear and all is green. You will find more pleasure—"

"Yes, yes," said the man.

"Raymond, don't cut him off." She sounded half-asleep.

"Look, I'm just—"

"Let me have the room key, will you?"

"But, I'll need it to—"

The woman blew a strand of hair out of her face and seemed to draw herself up on the seat. "I'm too tired to argue. Just give me the key. I need to get at my bag."

The man hesitated, then handed it over. The taxi departed. Mr. Gopti watched the man's eyes follow it. He winced once and then ran a hand across his mouth.

Mr. Gopti hailed another and the three of them got in.

A few miles later, they got back out on a nondescript street corner.

"Where's the bank?" said Raymond.

"Just over there." Roddy waved a hand. Palm trees obscured the view. "It is Indian bank. No foreigners there. It will look suspicious if you two are hanging about."

The Aussie was nodding in agreement.

"You give me cheques," said Roddy. "Wait here. My uncle will look them, give me money, and then we go to other bank."

"Wait a minute. I thought we—"

Jacko dug out some travelers' checks. "Don't worry, man. This is how we did it yesterday." He handed them over to Roddy.

"And your cash," said Roddy. Jacko produced a wad of bills. "How much is there?" said Roddy.

"Uh . . . eight hundred in cheques and two hundred in cash."

Roddy pocketed it and turned away. A moment later he was out of sight in the crowds.

Raymond stared at the Aussie. "You must be joking. You just

handed him all your money." He started after Roddy, but Jacko pulled him up. "No, no. Don't draw attention." He dug out some gum from a pocket and offered Raymond a stick.

Raymond declined, barely conscious of the offer. He was still staring in the direction Roddy had disappeared. "You just handed him your money. I'm not going to do that."

The Aussie chewed with vigor and pulled at the ends of his moustache. "This is what we did yesterday. He'll come back." He shrugged his broad shoulders and looked around. "I've always been a bit of a gambling man. I like a bit of risk." He looked at Raymond and smiled—just on the one side. "Nothing risked, nothing gained. Right?"

Raymond didn't respond. The fool, he was thinking. Just handed over his money. The checks could at least be replaced—unless they were already stolen, but the cash . . . What if Roddy didn't come back? What if . . .

And then Roddy reappeared. He was a little out of breath, but he was smiling. "Here is your money," he said, handing it back to the Aussie, who stuffed it quickly out of sight. "You should be more careful. You had two hundred twenty in cash, not two hundred." He laughed. Then he snapped out a five rupee note and gave it to the Aussie. "Get a cab and wait for us at the Taj Mahal."

Jacko waved down a taxi, got in, and was gone. Amazing, thought Raymond. The guy was honest.

"Okay," said Roddy. "Let me have your cheques."

Raymond found himself digging, almost automatically, into his pouch and produced a thick packet of travelers' checks. Their spurious origin seemed no longer of consequence. Twenty per cent of two thousand, he was thinking—and then, "Fourteen hundred," he said.

Roddy pocketed it. "And your cash."

Raymond was already pro-rating the four hundred out over days and weeks. Still on automatic pilot, he dug into the belt lining of his pants and brought forth the hidden roll of bills that he had carried all the way through Africa. He handed them to Roddy. "And six hundred in cash." His voice felt far away.

"Back in a moment." Roddy dove into the crowd. Raymond blinked and recovered himself. Better keep him in sight, he thought. As he moved toward the disappearing Roddy, a young Indian in western dress asked him for a light. "Don't smoke," he said and tried to wend his way through the crowd. Twenty percent of two grand—

"From where you are coming?" asked the chap with the unlit cigarette.

"Minnesota," he said absently, trying to squirm between the young man and two hunched-over coolies with loads of coal on their backs.

The young man barred his way, smiling. "Minnesota," he said. "Edmund Muskie."

"No, no. Gene McCarthy," Raymond countered and slipped under his arm.

The sidewalk was crowded with shoeshine boys, stray garbage, and a palsied beggar with an outstretched hand. Lines of women in brightly patterned *saris* moved slowly back and forth. Roddy was not in sight.

Raymond trotted along, dodging plops of cow dung and further beggars, but he could see it was hopeless to try and spot Roddy. He was out of sight.

Oh well, he told himself. He'd soon be back. Stop getting so nervous. He returned to his allotted corner and sat down on the stoop of a dry goods shop. After all, he'd had the Aussie's money and he'd returned. Raymond took comfort in that.

Time passed. It occurred to Raymond that the Aussie, after all, was no longer there. Neither was Adriana. He was isolated. He did one long, inner double take—the dumped checks and the African cash and the Aussie's one-sided smile and the long story about the family business spilling over into the remembered smell of that hotel pot of tea—and found himself swaying to his feet.

❊ ❊

Radhakrishnan Gopti was lingering over a double shot of Johnny

Walker Red and contemplating a take-out curry supper. He was feeling frisky, he decided, and well-earned it was too. Pity about the girl. He pulled his *dhoti* over his head, ran a hand over his pomaded hair, and stepped briskly through the door out of his sitting room.

Perhaps tomorrow—but then he shook off the thought. Tomorrow had troubles of its own.

He'd barely been allowed in the door of the Taj. The doorman—and the head desk clerk too, when called—were both quite certain. No unattended women had entered the building all day. Nor, for that matter, had any red-haired Australians with droopy moustaches.

And now, if sir would kindly move along towards the exit . . .

The Marathi lodging house had been a different matter, and a shock, even more, as Raymond had clung to the conviction that Adriana had opted to head straight for their stale little room as a result of her illness.

"Lady has gone, sar. Yes . . . yes, with bag. Most assuredly . . . not leaving key at present . . ."

He turned away then, and went out the door of the little hotel. For just a moment, the stale air seemed to cling to his skin, and then he was back in the hubbub of the streets outside.

He crossed over the road, oblivious to the horns and the bicycle bells and walked out along the shallow pier of the Gateway of India. A few beggars approached as he passed, but seeing the look in his eyes, made merely a silent, hopeless supplication and then withdrew.

At the end of the pier Raymond stopped, looking off across the waters colored by sludge and the muted gold of the falling sun. His mind had gone blank. He stood there at the edge of the sea, bereft of cunning.

Behind him, an arm plucked at his sleeve. "Sar, you want guide, sar? Very good. Number one." The weedy man with the huge bellbottoms.

For just a moment, a wild thought coursed through Raymond's mind. He would take the man on as partner. Ply the streets of Bombay until he found Roddy and that damned Australian—

He set the thought aside.

He'd been duped. Duped like a package cruise tourist fresh off the boat. And Adriana—he turned away from the edge of the pier, and brushed aside the insistent guide.

He had forty rupees in the pocket of his pants and a smallpox vaccination certificate that might bring twenty more. Enough for a day or two, but the future seemed not to matter just now.

Raymond took a step, and then another. His mind was no longer doing calculations. At the street end of the pier he turned south on a whim and began to walk, slowly and steadily, as if he had nothing else to do.

# WAITING FOR THE VOID

❈ ❈ ❈ ❈

SOMETIMES AT NIGHT, AINSLIE WOULD awake, sweating, and remember another piece of the life he had set aside. Never all of it, for who could remember all? But even the pieces—the bright, shiny slivers of the past that embedded themselves like weapons of torture inside his carefully cultivated fog of unknowing—were enough to leave him shaken and disturbed. He did not want them. He never sought them. They were lies that told a story that was no longer his. The old monk in Sukhothai had told it to him time and again: all that had come before was to be tossed aside; only the empty ones could enter the nulling void. And as he lay in a sudden fever heat, twisting on his little mat in the corner of Abadi's upper room, he would try to fend off the past by invoking the present.

He would listen, very carefully, for the rustlings of the geckos in their hiding holes in the roof. He would strain to hear the bending of reeds along the lakeshore or the call of a night bird in the *hariara* tree outside Abadi's yard. If he was fortunate, he might hear old Mama Rusli across the road up early, cooking her morning noodles to the hushed rhythm of her low-pitched hymn singing.

He would try to bring his whole mind to focus on the hearing of the sounds, but often (and he knew he could hardly expect otherwise) his mind would not obey. The old images would slide in—unwelcome guests at a party for one—and take the very seats of honor, brandishing their claims with a tenacity that left Ainslie gasping in its grip.

He would try to cry. But he never succeeded. It had been years since Ainslie had been able to cry. Not since the Brothers had taken him in from alongside the train line in Gujarat and he'd wept at the burden of life. Eventually, he would reach back inside the embroidered Tibetan shoulder bag hung from a peg along the wall of the darkened room and bring out his final solace. The little pipe and the resin box, sticky with the sweat of dreams. It might take an hour, he knew. Or more. But he could wait. He had nothing else to do . . .

Once it had been his mother's face, bending over him with a look of infinite tenderness as Ainslie offered up a bloodied hand, sliced by a bottle shard and dripping onto his knee. It was not the remembered wound that punctured Ainslie's fog, but the look his mother wore. He knew now that it was no more than a momentary surge of emotion—and emotion was a thing to be discarded like all the rest—but the memory of his own trust in its falsehood left a faint caress of warmth, as a blanket torn suddenly off will continue to heat the body for an instant, and that warmth made the deep inner chill all the harder to bear . . .

In the mornings, Abadi's wife brought him coffee and tapioca and asked after his desires for lunch. The proceedings were a formality, for there was never anything for lunch but *gado gado* and rice, but Ainslie held to the ritual with unswerving devotion. Its constancy lent him the illusion of choice within a prison of form—and in so doing, emptied his need to act.

Choice was something Ainslie both desired and feared. Indeed, the fear was of desire itself, that core of material being that still clung to him like a leaden weight suspended in the icy void. Choices did not exist, he told himself, and hoped that he would not dream of Harrison abandoned in the hut in the Karakorams.

The Harrison dream was particularly unsettling, for its outcome was uncertain. It began, always, with the smells of cooking grease over a dung fire and Harrison's bile upon the floor. The setting would appear whole: the smoke-blackened hut with the two rope-strung beds in the corners; the latrine hole outside the door; the view of the mountain, Rakaposhi, like a giant vulture hunched against the night sky. The weather was always the same. A pre-dawn chill that blew across the high valley with a hint of wetness thrown north by the monsoons that were whipping across the southern plains.

In the darkness, Ainslie could hear Harrison's retching. The thick, murky rasp was almost second nature by now; a counterpoint to every shared moment of the preceding weeks. Nothing could be done about it. Ainslie was certain of that. He had even called in the village doctor—a rheumy, one-eared man with a hennaed beard and two leather pouches of roots and powders. The doctor had flailed Harrison with pine boughs and smoked out the hut with a mixture of wood, herbs, and charcoal. When that failed he had proposed an exorcism whose effectiveness would be in proportion to its pain.

Ainslie had declined. Harrison—retching even then and moaning into the bed frame like a wounded cow—had been too weak to care.

It had taken Ainslie a week to arrange passage out. Only the tribesmen knew the trails and Ainslie, remembering the journey in, had not cared to flout their monopoly. Harrison, meanwhile, had begun to bring up blood.

That was how it had been on the still, starless morning when Ainslie slipped out of the hut, consigning Harrison to whatever god ruled the Karakoram range, but he had not reckoned on the recurrence of the dream.

That morning of departure had come only once. Why then must he be tormented over and over by its mere shadow—the internal dreamworld of a guilt he refused to acknowledge as worthy of the higher being? Why did this, too, not slip from him, as had the memories of childhood and joy and the other base temptations which the *bodhisattva* must laugh at from the welcoming void?

Mama Rusli visited Abadi's infrequently. Weeks might pass with Ainslie not seeing the nut-brown, withered face with the toothless smile. But not a day went by without him hearing her unsettling hymns. Worst was when the choir from Mama Rusli's church chose to practice in her yard. It was not that the singing was bad. Quite the contrary. It was full-throated and sinuous, like a civet cat calling to its mate with a longing no answer could ever quite suppress.

It was not the sound that bothered Ainslie. It was the emotion behind the sound which he found objectionable, like the church building itself—an absurd structure built around a European steeple, with a brass bell that some Dutchman had toted in a hundred years before.

There was no good reason, he felt, that these people should accept the religion of others. Surely it was the ways of their own ancestors that they were meant to follow. Not the headhunting portion of the legacy, perhaps, but the spiritual side. It was bad enough with Abadi, who occasionally sang along even while he shared the pipe on the timbered balcony overlooking the lake, but Mama Rusli had once gone so far as to press on Ainslie a small wooden cross which she said would knit his heart together once again.

He had laughed and asked her why she thought his heart needed knitting, but the old woman had only looked at the sky and pointed to the cloud cover, drifting in tendrils under the equatorial sun.

Ainslie had known there was no point in propounding to her his own philosophy of non-being, for had not the Buddha said that only the few might reach enlightenment and then only after the death of all desire?

But that night he'd had another dream . . .

It was Gujarat and the sharp edge of an Indian dusk had fallen on the banyan trees outside the village where Ainslie had come to die. At the well, the last gossipers had gathered up their jugs and the smell of cooking fires rose through the open windows of the huts beyond Ainslie's cloistered room. A peacock called from one of the trees, warning of the night, but Ainslie hardly heard. He was heating the bowl for the last time with the pellets he'd brought from Bombay.

The pungency of the cooking fires . . . the quiet murmur of the peasants as they broke and dipped their bread . . . the peacock calling—again now, urgent against the darkness . . . all this—an elemental cycle of uselessness—set the world's slow turning of doing and being and doing again to whirling in Ainslie's head like a circus pinwheel whose cheaply colored spokes refuse to disappear behind the bright gaiety of illusive movement.

It was all a sham. Pointless. There was no tomorrow. There had never been yesterday. There was only today, with its diminished possibilities and the cold loneliness of self-knowledge. Ainslie ached for the void. He went out of the room and down the muddy lane behind the town.

The peacock called again.

At the train tracks Ainslie sat down, weak and shaking, and waited for the Bombay Mail. The fog around him was thick and dulling. He lay his head down on something cold and waited . . .

Somewhere, the greyness had spilled into light, and from his mat in the upper room, Ainslie could hear a distant keening from the hut across the road. He knew he would not sleep again.

The keening rose in pitch. He recognized the choir members from Mama Rusli's church, but never had they practiced at this hour. He wiped his forehead for sweat and felt instead the cold that enveloped his limbs.

There were more singers across the road now. Chanting began to punctuate the sounds—a stiff, rhythmic intonation that brought back the funeral of a village elder which Ainslie had come upon once in the highlands beyond the lake. A night bird sang in the hariara tree and one of the chanters began to wail. Ainslie tried to pick out Mama Rusli's voice, but he could not.

He tried to sit up and failed. He lay still for a moment, straining to hear Mama Rusli's voice. It was not there . . . its absence an emptiness itself . . . and he knew at once for whom the current funeral was proceeding. The night bird called again.

Ainslie reached for the shoulder bag on its peg but his hand would not obey. He leaned back, rigid against the little mat, and shivered at the falling night.

# SOMETIMES

❄ ❄ ❄ ❄

Sometimes he thought about the old days.

Sometimes, especially when he was walking along the river late in the day, with the afternoon sun splashed over the trees on the western bank, the light would change and capture something—a gold-green glow reflected off the surface of the water—and suddenly it would be the Canal du Midi on a late summer day. A picnic on the banks. The boys skipping rocks and chasing each other along the tow path. His wife laid back in the deep grass that rose in waves up from the banks. A soft, ripening round of Camembert and the broken crusts of baguettes with all the time in the world to be eaten. The boys found a dead otter, or maybe it was a river rat, but something suitably rank, fly-buzzed in the reeds. A barge moved past in the distance, wash flapping on a line and a pig standing on the deck.

Why had that moment frozen, and not some other?

Then he remembered the tramp. The man had emerged from under the line of beech trees between the tow path and the upper road, limping steadily south and east, as the Canal bent in its journey down to the Mediterranean. His face had been lined, a week's growth of beard, eyes that looked everywhere and nowhere. A lumpy bit of pack on his back. He'd said nothing to the boys, just moved along steadily: limp, walk, limp. The boys had stopped their inspection of the water rat to study his back as he passed.

As he approached the adults, they could see the bulges in his pockets and the tatter to his coat. "*Je viens a la mer*," he said as he passed. "*Toujours la mer. Mais pourquoi? C'est tout la meme chose.*"

And then he trudged on. The boys wandered back, waving sticks and making faces over the smell of the dead rat. In the trees, a slight wind rustled leaves and then ran on across the far fields.

The light still held, but the moment slid on. As they gathered up the remains of the picnic lunch, and his wife began to talk of Carcassonne and the evening ahead, he held himself apart, just the littlest bit, thinking of the tramp . . . *Going to the sea, always the sea. But why? It was always the same thing.*

A moment here. A moment there. What did it matter? Why not a full flow of events? It wasn't that he couldn't remember. If anything, he remembered too much. That night in Carcassonne, for example.

The boys had discovered a tiny television up on the wall of their room in the *pension* and, after the long day on the road and in the sun, wanted nothing more than to lie on their bed and watch a movie, even if it was in French. A round of *croque monsieurs* and a liter of Citron had been obtained, along with instructions on how to find Madam Girard should anything untoward occur.

And then the two of them had set out for the lights of the castle down the road . . . Carcassonne, the vast and imaginatively reconstructed bastion that brooded over all the countryside around. Yet it wasn't the night inside the walls that slid into his memory banks—the crowds along the lanes, the unexpected conviviality of the cafe where they'd sat out in the square along with a mixed international host, the empty moat between the inner and outer walls where they'd walked, later, in near isolation—but rather the moment of returning to the pension. It was long into the night. They'd worried mildly about how the boys were coping. Then, as they stepped out of the car, she had inexplicably stood too close to her door as she went to close it, and managed to slam it straight into her forehead, eliciting a shriek and a curse, and the sudden scurrying of two sets of small feet onto the balcony outside their room. The boys, at least, were all right.

When they'd gotten her inside, there was a gash across her forehead and a line of blood dripping into her eye. Already the swelling had started. The worst of it was that an air of uncertainty seemed to hang over the event, as if he had been responsible for the accident; caused it even, or somehow provoked her into injury. They'd had a fine enough time in the soft city night, but now the end result was pain, and a bad memory of the brief moments snatched for themselves, as if they should feel guilty for momentarily abandoning the boys.

Sometimes, when he thought back hard enough, he wondered if that was the day it all went wrong. Or started to, anyway. Could you really single out a day? A moment? Was there a tipping point beyond which there was no going back?

Or was it just the memory of the tramp that sparked the connection?

He stood up then and shouldered his pack. The rest house was still several kilometers onward and he'd need his strength to start the climb through the Pyrenees tomorrow.

After that, the choice was his. Or so he liked to believe.

He wondered if the boys remembered that day along the Canal. He wondered if they still thought of him, at least from time to time. Then he moved off into the distance. Slow but steady. *A la mer*, he thought. *Toujours a la mer*.

# B-Side: Shifting Gears

✤✤✤✤

# JUMPING OFF

❊ ❊ ❊ ❊

SATURDAY IN THE RAIN, WITH heavy sluices of water running off my feet and the tired clop of four sodden shoes squishing along the sidewalk. Grandfather silent. Grandfather bundled inside his squeaking raincoat, bent under a brown cloth cap. Grandfather's hand tucked inside my arm. Mottled skin and thin, curling hairs along the knuckle where he grips, firm and trusting. Even in the rain he wears the sunglasses.

Squish, slop, squish, slop. Up another set of steps, onto the watersoaked welcome mat, ring the bell and wait. Smiling. Fixed, tight smiles. Me to say hello ma'am or hello is the lady of the house at home. Grandfather to start the pitch.

In the rain no one asks us in.

My box grows heavy. Cardboard wettening even under wraps and seeping like an infection down into the tight-packed goods. Christmas wrapping already in August. Some buy early, says Grandfather. Some wait just for me.

Down the steps, along the boulevard. Squish, slop, squish. My arm going numb. Baseball hat dripping rain off the bill and tightening along my forehead. Grandfather tall, but stooping. Faint smell of cheese clinging to his shirt, but covered now under the raincoat and the soft hiss of water sliding over the grass.

Gutters run with waste and leaves. A car splashes past. Up another set of steps. Ring the bell. Smiling.

Is the lady of the house at home?

The pitch.

Two dishcloths and a pot holder.

Are you really blind? she says.

Down the steps, along the street. Grandfather calculating in his head. Soft mutters and faint sucking of teeth. Turning the corner into a slash of wind. My eyes sting with rain. Grandfather grunts.

I think of him at night in the speckled brown chair worn smooth on the arms, with his feet up in tired slippers and the talking book on the phonograph. White hair in thinning strands. Shoulders slumped. Me crouching behind the sofa soft-tuning the radio to forbidden rock 'n' roll. Dead nights in Swedish parlors, with the clock ticking and Mormor in the kitchen. For treats, a glass of eggnog.

Mormor reading out evening news and sharing the parlor silence. Mormor packing the cardboard boxes and toting up the day's receipts. Driving the Chevrolet—perched up high and peering so she can see out over the hood. A tiny woman, stooped and hunched with age and aggravated injuries. Grandfather silent. Sucking on his teeth. Dreaming back to the years before the darkness fell.

Me vowing never to go blind. Never to tramp the streets of an indifferent city, begging the attention of gaping strangers. Never to sell or have to try to sell. Vowing aloofness. Vowing a better way.

The smell of Swedish meatballs and cooking potatoes hanging over the kitchen.

The clock ticking.

But now it is Saturday in the rain and my shoes squish on the grassy verge.

Up the steps, ring the bell. Smiling.
Nothing.
Down the steps, up the next. Smiling.
A box of birthday cards. A decorative spoon.
Down the steps . . .
Grandfather stumbling and coming aright. Grandfather leaning heavily on my shoulder as I see him on his days alone, cane tapping along the sidewalk like a metronome beating out a rhythm of need.
Down the steps.
Up another. No thank you.
Down the steps . . .
How do I know you're blind? she says.
Grandfather silent, but holding the smile.
Streets repeat. The wind shifts. Rain at our back pushing us forward. Grandfather's hand tucked inside my arm. Mottled skin and thin, curling hairs along the knuckle where he grips, tight, with a firmness that bonds like glue.
The box at my side is dragging. Evening is miles away. Grandfather sighs.
Up . . . down . . . smiling. Make the pitch. Never pressure.

Afterwards, in the car on the way home, Grandfather sucks on his teeth and counts the money. Does the calculations in his head, muttering softly as he counts, and then at the end, with every penny accounted for, he leans back to where I sit in the back seat and stretches his hand out toward mine.

Eighty-five, he says. Shows his teeth in that tight, fixed smile. Like something remembered from a distant past.

I take the coins held between his thumb and forefinger. Three quarters and a dime.

Then I sit way back on the old cloth seat and send my mind off on its fancies, willing it away from the gutter-slick streets. Away from the plain black Chevrolet. Away from Mormor, my tiny Swedish grandmother, perched on pillows so she can see out over the top of the steering wheel. Away from the repeating avenues of bungalows and back alleys. Away to wherever I can find to jump . . .

# GRANDFATHER AND THE FISH-GLOVE

❀ ❀ ❀ ❀

Even before I pull the old glove out from the packing box I know it is useless. It hangs off the end of my hand, drooping like a dead fish. I flap it once or twice, stretching to take the throw from short. The glove just twitches and leans towards the floor.

Billy Mueller gave it to me when he made the high school team. He said it was a Ferris Fain model but that the name got rubbed off. He said he knew it was awful old and probably too big, but it would do until I got another. Billy Mueller plays first base. He's left-handed too. I used to go to his house and he would give me pointers, but not any more. We moved and now all I've got is his glove. His old glove that is just two limp slabs of leather. It is useless.

A dead fish on the end of my hand.

It will never do. Not in this town. If they see me with this they will never let me play. I know it.

Last year, I was lucky. I was only nine and the first day when I came to practice wearing that glove everybody laughed, even the coach. But then Donnie Heisler, who lives down the block and is the fastest pitcher on the team, told the coach he should give me a chance. He said I knew what I was doing.

They put me on first base and I did okay, even with the fish-glove. Half the throws came on the bounce and I just stopped them with my knees. And Billy Mueller showed me how, if you hold your hand so the long slabs are aimed at the ground, you can catch balls right in the air. You have to make them hit just where your hand fits inside the glove and you have to slap your other hand right on top of the ball, but it works. Usually.

Donnie Heisler said anybody would miss throws like I got and besides, who did we have that was better. The coach made noises like a seal and flapped his arms. He is on the high school team, but I bet Billy Mueller is much better.

Anyway, that was last year. Now we live in Minnesota by a bunch of lakes and a printing plant where my dad works. Grandfather and Mormor live here too. They are very old and Swedish. He is blind. Every day he goes out and walks around from house to house selling things. Sometimes he has kids that lead him by the arm. Sometimes he just goes with a cane. When we visited them last summer, I led him around by the arm six different times and Grandfather told me the secret to getting respect was your shoes. He said if your shoes are scuffed, people will think you don't really care. It was a good thing he couldn't see my shoes.

He carries a big cardboard box with a rubber handle and whoever leads him by the arm carries a smaller box. Inside the boxes, Mormor puts all the stuff to sell, like wrapping paper and greeting cards, cake pans, dish cloths, cooking tools, and decorative Swedish sugar spoons. Grandfather also takes orders for brooms that some other blind people make in a factory somewhere. When Mormor comes to pick us up for lunch or supper, we have to go back to the right house and bring them their broom. It costs two dollars.

In the mornings we work from eight to twelve and you should wear a jacket because it's still chilly. You should also wear good comfortable shoes, because if you don't your feet will hurt and you will get bunions. That's what Grandfather said. When we walk I stand up as straight as I can so Grandfather can reach down and put his hand inside my arm. He can walk as fast as me but I don't think he can run.

I can run from first base to third as fast as anybody, Billy Mueller says. He showed me how to bend a little bit when you come near the base, so that you're aimed straight for the next one. And always touch the base with your right foot, he said. It's faster.

I tried to tell Grandfather that, but I don't think he understood. He asked me one day what was the most important thing I learned last year so I told him that about the bases, but he just sucked on his teeth and said when did we start to study geometry.

If you ask me, he never even played baseball. He used to be a business teacher before he went blind and probably he spent all his time doing arithmetic. He's awful good at it. At night when Mormor picks us up in the Chevrolet, Grandfather counts up all the money in his head and always gets it right. He keeps one-dollar bills in his pants pocket and fives and tens in his shirt. He folds them different ways so there's no mistake. He showed me how you tell pennies from dimes and nickels from quarters without looking. You rub your fingers along the rim and if there's no ridges it's a penny or a nickel. I used to do that as a trick in third grade during reading time but then Doreen McMillan figured out how and it wasn't very fun.

Another trick he showed me was how to do batting averages in your head real fast. He didn't mean for the trick to be batting averages that you would do, but that's how I use it. Last year I told everybody's batting average as soon as they came back to the bench from hitting, but then one time Buster Sikorski, who's supposed to be the best hitter, went 0-for-4 and said he would clean my clock if I announced any more batting averages, so I shut up.

If I do get to play baseball this year I will be happy not to have Buster Sikorski on the team. He always smelled like he needed a bath and when he put you in a headlock it stunk. Once I tried to hit him with my glove, and the coach said, "Throw him a fish! Throw him a fish!" and everybody laughed.

Everybody will laugh this year too if I try to play with that limp old fish-glove. Grandfather says not to pay any attention when people laugh at you because they are too small to know better. He says the same thing when people slam the door in our faces or make their dogs bark.

Not everybody is like that. Sometimes people give us water or iced tea. Once we went to the house of somebody he knew from church and we stayed there over an hour. We had mint cookies and strawberry punch, and I got to go play whiffle ball with their boy in the yard. He is one year older than me but not a very good baseball player. When I pitched the whiffle ball he could hardly hit it. When it was my turn I hit a liner into the kitchen window. Nothing got broke, but we had to stop playing and come inside.

Sometimes old ladies give me nickels. Once a lady gave me a quarter. I thought maybe she made a mistake and forgot to feel for the ridges around the rim of the coin. But I didn't say anything. I wanted to buy baseball cards, and you can get six packs for a quarter at Chlore's Store.

I wouldn't like to be blind. People look at you funny, like they think maybe you're cheating and can really see. Going around to houses selling things isn't so bad, but I would get tired of trying to find kids to lead me by the arm. I am useless with a cane.

I am also useless with this big old fish-glove, and if I do not get a new one I might as well be blind because I will not be able to play baseball this year. In this town, nobody goes down to the park to fool around and hit a few. All they care about is Little League. A real official Little League with uniforms and fences in the outfield.

I must definitely get a new glove. I can't ask my parents because they don't have a cent. I heard my dad tell my mom that only last week.

"The move took it all," he said.

"But Easter—"

"I don't care if it's the Queen's Jubilee," he said. "We don't have a red cent."

My birthday is not until August and by then the season will be over. I have eighteen dimes saved up in a jar, but you cannot buy a first baseman's glove for eighteen dimes. I have checked.

Ernie's Sporting Goods on Water Street has lots of first baseman's gloves. They smell like the buckskin shop we went in out West, and they have molded pockets so you would not even have to hold your hand pointing down to the ground. You could just give a good stretch—and snap—the ball would be there, stuck as tight as the gum on the bottom of the desks at school. The one I like best is smaller than the others. It's the color of Grandfather's Sunday shoes, and it says Stan Musial right in the pocket, clear as day. It costs $13.95, and Ernie told me he might be willing to make a deal on it, providing the right person wanted it.

I didn't ask him who the right person might be. The deal would never be for eighteen dimes.

At school everyone is talking about the Little League tryouts. They are only two weeks off, but I pretend not to care. Nobody asks me about them anyway. All I know is I do not want to be laughed at for trying to play while wearing a fish.

So I have thought up a plan. We have Easter vacation right before tryouts begin. What if I worked for Grandfather every day, morning and afternoon, for the whole week? Couldn't I earn enough money to buy the glove? When I add it up in my head, it seems to me that if I lived at Mormor and Grandfather's house all week and did not buy any baseball cards I could do it.

Anything is better than not getting to play ball all summer.

I wish I had never thought up my plan. Here it is, Friday afternoon and I have counted all my money three times and I still do not have nearly enough. Even worse, Easter vacation is almost over and I haven't been out to play ball once. After supper, I just read the box scores and do batting averages in my head. There is nothing else to do at Grandfather and Mormor's house except shine shoes. Grandfather has me shine his every night. Then he puts his feet up on a stool and reads his Bible in braille. Sometimes he listens to the radio or to his talking book. They don't have a TV. They don't have any books either, except big huge ones that are about business, or they're in Swedish.

I keep counting my money in my head while I lead Grandfather around. There's eighty-five cents for every morning session and eighty-five cents for every afternoon. There's also a nickel that a fat woman in a stained pink dress gave me, fifteen cents change that I got to keep when I delivered two dish cloths and a paring knife to Mrs. Svensen across the alley, and a dime and two pennies that I found on the sidewalk.

Now I walk with my eyes scanning the gutters for stray coins, and twice I've almost made Grandfather fall because I forgot to warn him about bumps in the pavement. Grandfather asks me what is wrong, but I don't know how to tell him. How can someone who is blind know what it feels like to watch a hardball go flying into your glove with a puff of dust? What good would it do to tell him anyway? He doesn't play baseball. He doesn't know the first thing about it.

Besides, it is too late. Even if I had enough money I would not have time to get used to the glove before tryouts begin. The other guys have been practicing all week, and I don't even have anyone to play catch with. My mom has to watch the little kids and, by the time my dad gets home, it is dark.

All afternoon, Grandfather keeps asking me what is the matter and finally I tell him. It takes a long time, and at the end when I stop he says I have overlooked one source of money.

I say, "What is that?"

He says, "It is the bonus given to any boy who leads me around all day every day for an entire week."

"You never told me about any bonus," I say.

"That is because nobody had ever done it until now."

I ask how much is the bonus and he says another day's wages.

Before I can even add it up he says that for a smart talker like me, that should be enough to make Ernie the sporting-goods man come to terms.

For two blocks, I am so happy that I don't even look for nickels on the sidewalk. Then I think about how stiff that new glove will be at first and how I don't have anybody to practice with and pretty soon I'm walking so slow that Grandfather asks me if I'm tired and need to sit down.

I explain about gloves when they're new and how a first baseman needs to have somebody who throws the ball to him, but Grandfather stops right in his tracks and puts his hand on my neck. "It is no different than life," he says. "It is all well and good to wait for somebody to throw you the ball, but what if they don't?"

I say, "Then the runner is safe."

He opens his mouth and then he shuts it. After that we don't talk much until it's almost time to go home and Grandfather says, "I bet some boys don't have any glove at all."

"I bet they don't play Little League either," I say.

"No, but they might do other things that are even more important."

I almost say, "Like what? Shine shoes?" but then we hear Mormor honking one long and two short and we don't talk any more.

When we get in the car Mormor tells him that he's scuffed his left shoe up bad and it's time he got a new pair. He tells her he's comfortable just the way he is. That new shoes never fit right anyway. They're too stiff. Mormor says stiff is better than shabby and since when did he stop caring about his shoes, but after that I don't listen. I sit in the back of the Chevrolet and count my money in my head and think about Grandfather and that old fish-glove.

When my mom picks me up I make her go straight to Ernie's Sporting Goods. I save back fifty cents and make a deal with Ernie on the Stan Musial glove. Then I show him my fifty cents and ask for a rubber ball. I figured out I could throw a rubber ball against our garage and it would bounce right back to me, almost like the throws in a game. It's not as good as having a friend to throw the ball, but it's a lot better than just sitting around wishing.

Sunday after church, I'm outside throwing when my mom comes out and says Grandfather called. I tell her I can't work for him this week because of tryouts, but she says that wasn't why he called. She says it's about his shoes.

"What shoes?" I say.

She says, "The new ones he just bought. I can't imagine why he's asking you, but he thinks they're too stiff and would you help him break them in? He'll be out here in an hour."

I want to say no because I need to practice, but Mom would only lecture me about gratitude and family and besides, my new glove is so stiff it makes my hand hurt just to flap the pocket.

When Grandfather and Mormor arrive, he stands next to where I'm throwing and listens to the ball plunk against the wooden slats of the garage. After a minute I stop throwing and lead him over to the steps so we can sit down and work on his shoes.

"There's a trick to new shoes," says Grandfather. He digs into his shoe bag, pulls the new pair out, and hands them across to me. "If you do not handle them right, they will never get properly broken in. But if you want to make the process proceed more rapidly—" he digs into the bag again, and this time he comes out with a mason jar half-filled with sticky goo, "—you rub this over them until they smell like pine cones melting in the sun."

I watch while Grandfather spreads the goo carefully over the surface of a shoe. His hand works the stickiness around and around in a circle and all the time he's pushing and prodding at the shoe with his other hand. Finally he stops. He says, "What do you think?"

"It doesn't look any different."

"It's not meant to," he says. "It's only the smell that changes." He holds the shoe up near my face. "Most folks do not really know how to smell properly, but if you can just not let your eyes get in the way, it should come through."

I inhale as deep as I can. Pine cones.

"Give it overnight," says Grandfather, "and that shoe will be as soft as your Mormor's satin pillow. Here, you do the other one."

I dip my hand in the goo and take his shoe, but I'm looking at the glove sitting on the steps beside me. "Grandfather," I say, "would this goo work on stuff besides shoes?"

"Probably not..."

"Oh."

"... unless it was leather," he says, and then he smiles.

I put down his shoe and pick up the Stan Musial glove, working at the pocket as I rub that goo over and over into the fresh leather. When I shut my eyes, I can see the throw coming in from short. Grandfather leans his head in close and together we sniff the pine cones, melting in the sun.

# A TOUCH OF THE WORD

❀ ❀ ❀ ❀

THE BIBLE WAS IN BRAILLE. The other books in my grandparents' house were all set in type, so far as I could ever discover. They stood tucked in place in the long, glass-enclosed bookcases that ran the length of the living room wall, back behind the radio cabinet and the overstuffed easy chairs with lace doilies pinned to the arms. There were textbooks on business law, faded hymnals, a boxed-set biography of Charles Finney, and entire rows of tattered, re-bound volumes in Swedish. There was even a tall, musty copy of *Grimm's Fairy Tales* that I used to sneak out of its spot on the lower shelf, just next to *Pilgrim's Progress*. It had been printed in London in 1882 and I would curl myself up there on the floor, behind the green horsehair rocker, to pore over the Victorian illustrations whose celebration of death and horror I found both captivating and terrifying. But only the Bible was in braille.

In the evenings, after the day's accounts had been seen to and the rubber-handled boxes had been packed up tight for the next day's selling with greeting cards, cake pans, dishcloths, decorative Swedish sugar spoons, and the like, Mormor would sit down at the tatty end of the sofa and read the newspaper aloud. Grandfather would sit in silence for the most part, sucking at his teeth or grunting from time to time, and then at the end he would say, "Thank you, dearie," and Mormor would return to the kitchen.

Then Grandfather's feet—still swollen from the long day's walking—would go up on his footstool and his head would lean back in his chair. He wasn't asleep. He was only musing.

He might be counting up the day's receipts again in his head. He might be rethinking his sales pitch or wondering why paring knives had ceased to move. He might even be asking himself, deep in his heart of hearts, whether his entire previous career as a professor of business had been but a prelude to this moment. Whether the exchange of theory for practice had been preordained. A lesser man might have questioned whose purpose it served to strip a sober, industrious Swede of his livelihood and send him out on the streets—well past retirement age—to plod the boulevards and back alleys looking for a sale. A lesser man might have questioned the onset of blindness. But not Grandfather. He knew whose purpose it served.

That's why the Bible was in braille.

After he'd finished his musings, Grandfather would take it down from the shelf, carefully and with both hands on the spine, and lay it out flat on his lap. From behind the green horsehair rocking chair—wide-eyed over *Grimm's* or hunting stray rock 'n' roll tunes whispering in through the ether—I would crouch in stillness, watching and wondering at the hold the great book had over him. The ritual was unchanging.

He'd run his hand first over the cover. Soft, pebbled Moroccan leather gone limp with age and smelling of the hand that stroked it. Then he'd feel along the side, opening the yellowed pages to the chapter of his choice, and begin to run his fingers over the upraised dots.

Often he began in a hurry. The thin, curling hairs along his knuckles would catch the light as they moved and the opening lines would fly past in a flurry of terse, flicking movements. Then a phrase would catch his attention—a parable, perhaps, or a dictum that required consideration—and the flicking would slow to a measured, rhythmic pace.

From my spot behind the horsehair rocker, I would watch, certain of being unseen. Gradually, the lines of his forehead would soften and disappear. The stiffness in his legs—harbingers of a phlebitis yet to come—would ease. I knew then that he was about to enter the presence of his living God.

It would come upon him slowly, like the distant drone of static that beamed in when I turned on the old tube radio. You could see it in his fingers. The measured, rhythmic pace would fade to a long, slow stroking of the upraised dots. A caress almost, of the living, touchable Word. Such a different feeling than the one I got when I read books; when there was always a separateness between myself and the words on the page. Other books required a mental leap to get from printed type to eye level comprehension. Grandfather's Bible—huge and cumbersome as it was, with its patterned spots and double-width pages—required no such mid-air jump. Wisdom . . . insights . . . truth . . . these flowed directly into his fingers and up through his body, permeating him with a directness that could not be duplicated by eye.

How much I understood of this, at first, would be hard to say. But the memory of the smooth-stroking fingers stayed with me and the idea of a hidden code that could unlock the precious truths of the Word of God worked away at my soul. In the night, awakening from death-dreams set off by pictures of the Brothers Grimm, I would still my racing heart by conjuring the sweep of Grandfather's hand on the dotted parchments.

I did not speak to him of this. But I watched: the ritual of touching the outer cover; the selection of chapter and verse; the first beginning lines flicked over and then the long, slow swell of silent communion with the secrets of a great and terrifying Lord.

For a long time I was content merely to watch. But as I grew older, the sensuousness of those stroking fingers—the obvious pleasure in the feel of the words—the very potential for physicality in the Word of God—began to take hold of my imagination.

I, too, wanted access to the divine. I, too, wanted the great sea of epiphany to swell inside my soul. That this might come in a deeply physical sense seemed only natural. I had not yet learned the practice of separating body from spirit. But I knew no other gateway—only the Bible that was in braille.

When I visited my grandparents, I began to make a point of touching the Bible. I would wait until I was alone in the living room and then run my fingers over passages that I knew by heart ("In the beginning, God . . ."; "The Lord is my shepherd . . ."), feeling for the connection I'd seen my grandfather make. I never told him about it. Perhaps I had some notion that he would resent another hand laid upon his book. Perhaps I was ashamed.

In any case, the connection eluded me.

Time went by. I entered Junior High and, with it, Confirmation studies at my local church. We examined the problem of pain and of unmerited suffering. Not surprisingly, my thoughts went quickly to the old ones—to my longsuffering Swedish grandparents, so seemingly inured to the injustice of their world. I began, at first, to be skeptical, and then to be angry. The catechisms we learned—the creeds, the formulas, the oft-repeated proof texts—seemed far removed from life.

They might well be true, I knew, but they didn't touch me where it hurt. They only left me wondering, cold, and uncertain as to whether blindness was a scourge or a gift so subtle it could be entrusted to only a few.

Now when I visited my grandparents' house, I saw too clearly the pinched, diminished circumstances under which they lived. I no longer desired to fondle the heavy leather Bible set next to my grandfather's chair. I was too aware of the painful clump of Mormor's hobbled feet; too aware of the necessity of small frugalities or the shaking in Grandfather's mottled hands. Yet still, I never heard them complain. Not about the continued long hours of selling on foot—come rain, shine, or indifference.

Not about the cruel jokes sometimes played by the ignorant. Not about the nights when Mormor drove to their appointed rendezvous and Grandfather wasn't there, having taken a wrong turn sometime in the day and wandered off at odd angles into the city, bumping his way along the curb and fending off dogs with his cane.

What was I missing? What did they have that I did not? I refused to ask, and if Grandfather sensed my disturbance he gave no sign. He still tucked his feet up on his stool in the evening. Still ran his fingers over the upraised dots. And on even the foulest of nights—with winter like a sword in the lungs, or the day's take a matter of change—his brow still softened and the stiffness still eased, though sometimes, now, the stroking went on for hours.

I was too young to know that he was dying.

I knew only that his life was not the one he deserved, and on an evening in May, a matter of days before I was to take my place on the stand with the other confirmands, my young will rebelled and I refused to go through with the ceremony.

The details hardly matter. The long harangues with my parents, the shouting match in the pastor's study . . . these were merely pinpricks raised over a surface of grief. I was angry at every prospect of life and to sacrifice the gown, the ceremony, and the traditional, personally engraved confirmand's Bible seemed fitting, even if ultimately pointless.

I was making a statement and make it, I did. I never explained myself to my grandparents, and they, as I expected, never raised my rebellion as an issue. When next I visited, Grandfather was unable to stand up. I took his hand and held it in silence for a long, long moment. Thin, curling hairs along the knuckles. Mottled spots like teardrops on the skin. Old hands worn smooth and sensitive by the passing of pages beneath. Could he feel in them my questions? Could he know my doubts through his fingertips? I didn't ask.

Six weeks later, he was dead.

At the funeral, Mormor had to be helped down the aisle in

a walker and, afterwards, it fell to me to see her up her steps and safely home. There at the door, entering the heavy silence of the empty house, she turned and handed me a book that had been laying on the entry table.

"We felt you needed a Bible of your own," she said. "I know you didn't get one at Confirmation."

I mumbled something in reply.

"I told him that you should have the same as the others received, but he insisted. Some are like Thomas, he said. Some must touch the nail prints and feel the wound in the side."

I picked up the cumbersome book and ran my fingers slowly over the pebbled surface of its cover. The smell of honest sweat still mingled with the rich scent of Moroccan leather, and for a moment, I felt very old.

"A Bible of your own," she said.

# THE BOOTS OF ALFRED BETTINGDORF

ALFRED BETTINGDORF WAS A FIRST-CLASS twit. Twit, dork, squirrel, lead brain, shite-tooth: you name it, Alfred got called it. He slunk down the halls of our high school with a perpetual look of hunted malice. He hardly ever made it between classes without at least one unprovoked shove or verbal taunt. Yet he never retaliated. He'd just squint his beady eyes and shove his double-thick glasses further up his nose and bumble on in silence.

I was never one of his abusers. I don't say that to pat myself on the back; it's just that to me, guys like Alfred were too pathetic to attack. I tended to ignore him, as much out of embarrassment at his awkwardness as anything else.

Besides, I had other things to fret about. Like Suzie Sutton. Now there are pretty girls and *pretty* girls. But in 1964, as far as I was concerned, there was only Suzie Sutton. My eyes were blinded to all else. I saw her in my study hall daydreams . . . I saw her while I bounced along in the back of the school bus . . . I even saw her on the blackboard while the math teacher drew sine waves and bell curves. I was gone.

Not that I was the only one so afflicted. Suzie had the kind of build that made the physics teacher fumble for his slide rule: mathematical perfection with a jiggle and a swish. She had long black hair that rippled in the wind, and eyes to match. Not dark. Black. Raven black. Suzie knew what she had, too—and just how to use it. Half the school was hot on her (the other half were girls, and probably a few of them shared the heat), but she always managed to keep her suitors panting in a pack.

In order to see her, I contrived elaborate routes between classes and after school. I knew her class schedule by heart, her locker number, where she met her friends. I even knew how many times she went to the john. When the bell rang to end a class I would dash madly to a selected point and then loiter there (still puffing from my run), casually adjusting the three-finger collar of my tailored shirt, staring out of the corner of my eye while she swirled past, surrounded by her circle of friends.

Oh, the joys that could be wrenched from a glimpse of those blood red lips, a passing fragrance from her hair! And then when she'd passed, a last lingering stare at her hips swaying on so fine and free above those achingly long legs . . . Then another bell would ring and I'd limp into my next class.

Our school was an old brownstone affair: two-storied, institutional. The floors were wooden and creaked when trod upon. This made skipping classes somewhat difficult, as even the lightest tiptoe set the boards to sounding up and down the hallway. The only people who could move with impunity through the halls during class hours were debaters and a few selected jocks. Debaters, because they looked so glum and studious that nobody could imagine they were up to anything wrong. The jocks, because they were heroes to the school at large—teachers included—and heroes, they tell me, are hard to find. Whenever confronted by authority, the jocks swaggered a little bit harder and mumbled something about "Coach wants to see me" and they'd be waved on.

As autumn's winds bared the branches outside, a new wrinkle in hallway freedom developed. There was to be an All-School Talent Show, and those who volunteered to help prepare for it were allowed out of class. I didn't help, of course, but I took to carrying a couple of posters and an extra notebook around as cover for my own excursions.

I was still on the trail of Suzie Sutton, and grabbed at any excuse for better viewing or a potential opportunity for contact. The second-storey windows on the south side of the building looked out over the school parking lot and it was from these windows that I bade farewell each day to the elusive Miss Sutton. I was so caught up in watching her that it took a while for me to realize how often I was seeing Alfred Bettingdorf. At first I figured it was coincidence, or just the fact that Alfred's gawky frame attracted attention wherever he went.

Then one day I finally realized what was up. Having just seen Suzie off for home in her pink Mustang (from a distance, of course), I turned away from my window vantage point and there was Alfred Bettingdorf lurking in a corner, licking his lips and still staring out at the parking lot. The hall was empty.

An instant flash told me Alfred—poor, puny, pathetic little Alfred—was hung up on the same chick I was. Against all reason, I felt a momentary bond of friendship.

I looked at him as I passed. He shied away, covering his torso with his notebook. That got to me. I stopped and his eyes narrowed. He kept his body covered. "She's something else, ain't she, Alfred?" My levity was forced.

He licked at his lips and said, "I got a right to watch," in his perpetual whine.

"Did I say you didn't? That's all you'll ever get to do, though." Suddenly I felt low and I turned to leave.

"Same with you." He barely breathed it out.

I stopped and looked back. He swallowed and spoke—no whine this time, just a bit of falter. "I mean . . . you watch her too. You never get any closer."

It dawned on me that it would look very bad for my reputation if this fact were discovered. I crooked a finger towards Alfred. Instinctively, he cowered. "That's between you and me, buddy. Understand?"

He nodded violently, glasses bobbing on his nose. I departed.

That was the end of it as far as I was concerned. But Alfred had the same English class as I did. Two days later, old lady Olafson gave us a writing assignment. I knocked out some drudgery about life in a caddy shack and got the speechifying over as quickly as possible.

When it was Alfred's turn, he stood up to a muted chorus of hoots. Olafson glared for silence. Alfred stood knock-kneed at the podium pushing at the heavy glasses that slid down his lengthy nose.

He cleared his throat and from the back row Milnor imitated a seal. Alfred's cheeks reddened. Then, with a grim, determined set to his face he began to read.

> Eddie was born in a laundromat,
> or at least that's what he thought.
> He spent his days by the big machines
> where his parents worked and fought.
> A ten–foot counter, a two-tiered shelf
> and sixteen machines in a line.
> Eddie knew the scene like the back of his hand.
> It was staring at him all of the time.

Alfred paused and caught his breath. Amazingly, the room was quiet. He went on faster, thick lips framing an uneven row of teeth and a thin stream of spittle spewing forth on the sibilants.

> They said, "the boy's in the basement
> the boy's hiding out back . . .
> now what you gonna do
> with a boy like that?"

Daddy was grey, kinda tired and fat.
And Ma, she had straggly hair . . ."

What was this stuff? It sounded like a song, and not a bad one at that. I sat up straighter, tapping my foot to the cadence. The room was no longer quiet, and except for me and old lady Olafson grim-faced in a corner, Alfred seemed to have lost his audience.

. . . The street outside was a world apart,
left for bullies and groceries and school . . .

They said, 'the boy's not in bed yet
the boy's getting fat . . .
now what you gonna do
with a boy like that?'

Alfred stuttered, losing the beat and finally stumbled to a halt. He wiped his mouth with the back of his hand and walked quickly down the aisle towards me, gripping the sheets of paper he'd been reading from and staring at his shoes. Olafson was already lambasting the loudest talkers and calling for the next volunteer, so I grabbed Alfred as he went by. Attention had turned to the front, where Big Brenda Phillips was still jiggling slightly from her passage to the front.

"Alfred, you write that stuff yourself?"

He blinked rapidly. "Sh-sh-sure," he said in a whisper. "I . . . I write lots of stuff."

I looked at him with a cold eye, still not quite believing.

"Really," he said. "I got the idea from 'Grown Up Wrong.' Off the new Stones album."

"The what?"

"The new Stones album. Look." He ducked over to his seat and under cover of Big Brenda's chesty mew, scooted back and slipped a record jacket into my hands. I glanced towards Olafson's desk in the front corner of the room. She was occupied.

I turned the album around in my hands. "Where'd you get this? I never saw this one."

"It's just out. Called *12 X 5*. It's great. Even better than their first." Alfred's hiss rose in volume as his enthusiasm swelled.

I glanced back at the front. The teacher was still occupied. "You a Stones fan?" It just didn't fit.

"Hey, yeah. Yeah, definitely." Alfred's eyes (as much as I could see of them through his glasses) gleamed. His voice rose. "Yeah. I play guitar and—"

"Sykes. Bettingdorf. What's going on over there?" A harsh voice from the front. Old lady Olafson stood up and peered out at us. Alfred shrank backwards. "No personal conversation, you two. Save it for after class."

Scattered sniggers and a warbled "Bettingdorf-dorf-dorf—" trailed Alfred back to his seat.

My ears burned. My name had been publicly linked with his. I, Gabe Sykes, seemingly suave of dress and demeanor, publicly linked with scrawny, rumpled-shirted Alfred Bettingdorf. That he could write song lyrics seemed little consolation. His status was nil. I kept my eyes down on my desk, desperately hoping the incident would be forgotten.

My eyes focused. The Stones record still lay in front of me. A new one! I'd just about played the grooves off their first: *England's Newest Hitmakers*. A new Stones album! This was an event. I stared at the cover photo, imagining myself as Brian Jones. Blond and beautiful, hippest of the hip. I watched myself striding haughtily past Suzie Sutton, felt her tugging on my arm, begging for attention. A new Stones album!

The bell rang.

I had to hear it. Against my better judgment, against all social sense, I approached Alfred. He was smiling again, those strange full lips curled around his off-white teeth.

I held up the album. "Mind if I borrow this overnight? I got to hear this. I'll bring it back tomorrow, no sweat."

He scratched at his nose. "Yeah, you can borrow it. But just one night, you hear?"

I was already gone into the crowd of departing students. But I heard. I just didn't want our faces imprinted together in anybody's mind.

❁ ❁

Alfred was right. The album was great. "Under the Boardwalk" was an instant favorite. I lay up in my bedroom and just let the needle drop back on it over and over. If I were Brian Jones, I thought. I lay there imagining myself stretched out at seaside with Suzie's black eyes flashing into mine and the world going by somewhere at a distance. If I were Brian Jones . . .

❁ ❁

The next morning, I was watching the pink Mustang pull into the parking lot when I spotted an odd-looking shirt out of the corner of my eye. It was Alfred.

"What'd you think of the album?" His grin was wide and goofy.

"Uh, good stuff, Alfred. Good stuff. Just a sec." We both paused and watched as a lithe figure with raven tresses whipping in the wind came strutting across the parking lot. Alfred sighed. I had more composure, but I felt the same. I turned away from the window.

Never any closer. Never anything more than a passing glance. Not a smile, not a touch, not even a sign of recognition. Hopeless. I felt at that moment as much a twit as Alfred.

After a moment of silence I handed back the album.

"Like my shirt?" said Alfred proudly. I watched his little chest expand.

"Well . . ." I hesitated. Might as well tell him. "Tab collars just don't make it, Alfred." I said it as gently as I could. I was still feeling blue over Suzie.

"Oh yeah?" His eyes flashed. "Jagger's wearing one. Look there." He pointed at the cover. Sure enough. "You telling me the Stones don't make it?" Damn. Sure enough.

It hit me in a flash. Provincials. We were all provincials. Our whole fashion pattern, the entire intricate structure of proper high school hipster wear—built on the basic truth of the three-finger button-down collar, was all provincial. Arbitrary, conservative. I looked more closely at the picture of the Stones. Richards, Watts, none of them wore three-finger button-downs. Jones—Brian Jones—was wearing a flyaway collar! No buttons at all. A flyaway! My universe teetered. My hand shook. Then I focused and held firm.

I looked back at Alfred. He pushed his glasses up on his nose. His eyes looked different, more piercing. For the first time I saw a bit of what lurked beneath them. Hidden there, under all the fear and pain of being perpetually tormented, I saw an awareness of the forces—the capricious, herd-like forces—that bound and dictated our habits.

I stared. He blinked.

"Look at this." He pulled out a magazine photo of the Stones: a full-length shot. "Look at those shoes," he said. "You ever see anybody around here wear shoes like that?"

Richards wore boots. Scruffy, black, pointy-toed boots that disappeared up under his pants. Jagger had on what looked to be white hush puppies. Both were a far cry from the round-toed spit-shined wing tips that dominated our hallways.

"I'm gonna get me a pair of boots," he said. "Even if nobody else knows, at least I will. I'm gonna wear them for the Talent Show."

I was still trying to rein in my racing thoughts. Provincials. Conservatives. Or . . . could it just be that nobody had the nerve to pick up on what was new? Could it be that this was how fashion changed? That one day an Alfred Bettingdorf saw a picture on a record and took a chance at being laughed at?

It was too much to swallow. I handed the picture back. "Sounds good, Alfred. Why don't you try that?" Still dazed, I started off down the hall.

Alfred called after me. "Gabe," he said, and I stopped. "I understand. It's harder for you. They don't laugh at you." He pushed his glasses up. "Me? I got nothing to lose."

I went on to study hall in a fog. There was a math quiz coming up that needed prompt attention, but I stared blankly at the same page for the rest of the hour. I wondered what Buddy Holly had looked like when he was in high school. A gawky kid with huge specs and a nasal voice. Or Jagger. Even Jagger. I remembered reading an interview where he said that when he was growing up he never knew if he was extraordinarily ugly or not. Those oversized lips, the sinuous curl of red against his teeth, a gash in his face almost as bad as Alf—I stopped. I had been about to say almost as bad as Alfred Bettingdorf.

At lunch that day, everybody was talking about the Talent Show. The list of performers had finally been posted. I dropped my food tray on the table next to Jimmy Spees and sat down. Jacobson and the boys were roaring with laughter across from us.

"What's so funny, Jake?" I asked.

"Tell it again, Jake," said somebody at his side.

He stopped in mid-guffaw. "They left off one of the performer's names," he said. "Suzie Sutton. Check this for an act. She comes out with just a bikini, a whip, and a trained German shepherd. And a little background music, like maybe "Ain't Too Proud to Beg." And then she starts . . ."

I tried not to listen. Jacobson always was a little too graphic for me. I hummed to myself 'til I heard more bursts of laughter.

"Hey, Jimmy," I said. "Who *is* performing?"

He shoved a list my way and I scanned it fast. "No real surprises there."

"Except one," he said. "Look there. Madcap & the Laughs. Now who the heck is that? Only bands in this school are the Disasters and the Falling Rocks."

He was right. Nobody seemed to know who they were. Even the heaviest gossips were stumped. For a day or so, it was topic number one. Then I went back to thinking about more important things, like the way to Suzie Sutton's heart. Assuming there was one. She sure didn't seem to make very many people happy. I guess when you're beautiful you don't have to.

The following Monday, Alfred appeared in his new boots. "Had to go thirty miles to get these," he told me. "Nobody's got them like this around here."

He paid for his daring. After third hour a couple of the jocks noticed his footgear. By the end of the day they had half the senior class participating in a new game—step on Alfred's boots.

He wasn't at the window watching the pink Mustang depart that night and he wasn't at school at all the next day. When I saw him again, he was limping, and the boots were a mess. But he still wore them. And that hunted look in his eyes had been replaced by a sharp defiance, obvious immediately to anybody who cared to look. Few did.

"I beat them," he said. "Every one of them."

"How's that? Seems to me they got you."

"Uh-uh." He pointed at his feet. "I'm still wearing them, right? They had their fun, they did their damage. But I'm still wearing them. And now the laugh's on them." His lip curled in a sneer.

I pulled doubtfully at my earlobe.

Alfred's fists clenched and unclenched. "Don't you see? One day they'll be wearing them too. And on that day they'll have to suffer with the fact that I—I, Alfred Bettingdorf—was wearing them first." He ran his fingers through his hair. "I'm letting my hair grow too. And practicing . . . every day."

"Practicing?"

"Guitar. I been telling you. I'm gonna enter that Talent Show. You just wait and see what happens."

"It's too late, Alfred." I really felt sorry for him now. Him and his delusions. "They've already got a full list."

"I know. I'm on it." He lowered his head and looked at me over his glasses. "We're Madcap & the Laughs."

"What!" I jerked back a step. "You mean it? You're the unknown band?"

"Well, not me alone. Got a couple of buddies from Central High who've been playing around together. It's a three piece."

Alfred with buddies . . . in a band? This was more than I could process. This was definitely too much. Again I flashed on Buddy Holly.

"Alfred, they'll laugh you out of town. You know that."

He snorted. "So what's new. I been laughed at all my life. At least I'll know, even if no one else does. I'm gonna show those jocks. I'm gonna show Jacobson and Milnor and all those guys." His eyes were wide and glaring through his glasses. "And I'm gonna show that Suzie Sutton," he said. "I'm gonna show her she ain't the only thing going." His whole body was vibrating with excitement. "I gotta go."

He turned and ran down the hall, the clumping of his boots drowning out the creaking of the wooden floor.

I watched him go. Then I stood at the window for a long time while the cars pulled out one by one from the parking lot. The pink Mustang was still there. My stomach churned, sickness deep in my loins. I felt rash and desperate and ready for anything.

I straightened my three-finger collar and shined my cordovan wing tips on the back of my pant legs. I took a step, then another. The floor creaked beneath me. I was walking steadily now, heart thumping, palms wet with sweat.

I caught up with her at the door of her car.

"Uh, Suzie. You got a sec?" My voice sounded hoarse and weak. I cleared my throat.

She turned towards me in a swirl of ebony locks. A musky fragrance enveloped my head and I fought off dizziness.

"Yes?" she said, head cocked seductively at an angle. It was the first word she'd ever spoken to me.

"Uh . . . I was wondering . . ." I flashed my biggest smile. "I was wondering if you'd go to the Talent Show with me?"

There was a second of silence; an endless, heart-thumping

second while we stood staring at each other. Her eyes burned into mine with black intensity. Then she grimaced, and laughed. "Go with you?" she said. "You must be joking."

She opened the car door, got in, and was gone in an instant. I stood frozen to the spot, smile iced in place. Mercifully, I was numb. Except for the huge hunk of lead that clogged my throat.

I walked home that night. It took two and a half hours, but I didn't care. Anything to keep from existing. I told my mother I was sick and went straight to bed. The lead in my throat had passed to my stomach and I wondered if I could ever eat another meal. I considered flinging myself under a truck, or joining the navy. I knew I would never go to school again.

Towards dawn I thought of Alfred Bettingdorf. How often had he laid like this, victim of unbearable humiliation? Still sleepless, equal parts rage and shame, I switched on the radio. They were playing the new Stones' single, "Time Is On My Side."

Alfred and those crazy boots. I rolled over and went to sleep.

Everybody went to the Talent Show. Numerous parties were scheduled for afterwards. Jimmy Spees knew of one at some girl's house and Jacobson was having a kegger down by the river. I felt like getting wild.

The acts were nothing special. A thin, anemic senior girl played Chopin to yawns and twitching. The football team did a silly skit about cheerleaders. There were two bad comedians and some very ordinary rock 'n' roll from the Disasters.

Suzie and her friends held center stage most of the night. Prancing and posing like uncrowned royalty, they whirled in a ceaseless circuit of male attention. I felt sick to my stomach just watching, but still the attraction was there. I knew what they said about the spider and fly—but knowing it didn't help.

Madcap & the Laughs were scheduled last. I was certain Alfred would be pathetic, but I felt I owed it to him to stay and watch.

The lights dimmed. The MC shouted "Madcap & the Laughs," and there they were churning their way through "Time Is On My Side." A well-pimpled boy with long bangs beat out a rough-and-ready rhythm on his drums. The bassman was a hollow-faced fellow whose cheeks expanded and contracted in a soundless parallel to the song's tempo.

But Alfred—Alfred Bettingdorf, first-class twit—was everybody's focus of attention. His hair was combed down in his eyes and he'd left his glasses at home. I doubt he could see beyond his mike stand. He wore a tab collar shirt and a vest that looked like something off the cover of *England's Newest Hitmakers*. And his toes tapped rhythm in scuffed black boots that disappeared up the leg of his pants.

Alfred could play. He was no Keith Richards, and his voice bore little resemblance to Jagger's, but he had the phrasing down—and he knew exactly how it all should look.

I was astounded.

They banged to a halt and went into something new, something I couldn't recognize. Alfred shook his hair as he sang. And then I realized I'd heard those words before:

> They said, 'the boy's in the basement,
> the boy's hiding out back.
> Now what you gonna do
> with a boy like that'

It was an Alf original. The one he'd read in Olafson's English class. The arrangement was more than the band could handle, but still—this thing kicked. Suzie and her crowd were pointing and making faces, oblivious to anything but their own safe standards of hipness. She was up near the front of the stage, wearing a patrician sneer, when Alfred suddenly stomped his foot and the band changed gears.

It was another Stones song, the final cut on *12 X 5*: "Suzie Q." That took nerve. I looked over to where Suzie stood, wondering what she thought. She was laughing; openly, shamelessly laughing. One of her friends mimicked Alfred—but not nearly as well as Alfred was mimicking Jagger.

Then Alfred, bat-eyed and nerveless, picked out that mass of raven black hair from the crowd and sang straight at it.

Suzie's laughter froze, and under his strutting, near-sighted, saliva-spewing spell, her smile vanished. He was singing to her. In front of a crowd. "Oh, Suzie Q," wailed Alfred in a guttural drawl, drawing his lips thickly around his teeth, "Tell me, who needs you?"

His own words again!

She shrank back into the wall and edged along it towards the rear, her haughtiness tempered momentarily with shame.

I looked at the rest of the crowd. Everybody seemed to think it was a joke—Alfred Bettingdorf, always good for a laugh. Nobody paid it much attention, except to ridicule. Couldn't they see? Couldn't they hear? This kid had something. Rough, yes. Derivative, certainly. But here was raw talent far above whatever else we'd been watching. But nobody noticed. They couldn't see past Alfred Bettingdorf, first-class twit.

The Laughs stopped. A few hands clapped. Far more stayed in pockets while their owners jeered. The lights came up and the show was over. I suddenly realized I didn't feel like partying. Not at all.

I walked up to the stage, with Suzie and her crowd alongside. I barely noticed. Alfred was putting his guitar back in its case. Suzie pushed past me and stood staring for a moment at Alfred, her fists clasping and unclasping. "Creep," she snapped. Alfred smiled into the case.

She turned away again, and the ugly set to her mouth softened into a vast, insincere smile. She waved across at somebody on the far wall and her whole retinue of camp followers departed in her wake.

I waited until the stage area cleared and Alfred was locking his case. "Alf," I said. "Hey, Alf."

He blinked vaguely towards me. "That you, Gabe?"

"Alf, that was incredible. You've got Jagger down cold. You're a performer."

He blushed and kicked the floor with his foot. "Thanks. I'm glad somebody knows."

We stood there for a minute.

"I heard of a party Suzie Sutton's going to," he said at last. "I got no hope, but you could probably get in."

I looked behind me to where she was sweeping grandly out of the room. "No," I said. "I don't think so. I got other things to do." I stood there a minute, thinking. "Say Alf, where did you say you got those boots?"

# A ROCKER'S GUIDE TO THE HISTORY OF THE FUTURE
## (VERSION '81)

IT WAS THE TIME OF the Troubles then, but near the beginning, before everybody took to the streets. The Sound Bans had been out for nearly two years and whatever music we got, we got on the lam.

The Bans had been a surprise announcement by the newly formed Department of Internal Security. Certain forms of music, we were told, had detrimental consequences for both personal and social integration. As such, these forms had no right of access to public airwaves. Overnight, the radio became a beacon of Easy Listening.

Then came the exemptions. Classical music was exonerated *a priori*. Disco was cleared for use as an aid to physical conditioning and religious hymns were allowed to be broadcast at private expense provided a warning as to the presence of "inherent spiritual content" was aired in advance. It took a special act of Congress to clear Country & Western—and even that battle was won only after the threat of a filibuster by the senators from Tennessee.

In the end, the targets were obvious: most black music styles and . . . rock 'n' roll.

❀ ❀

I'd been working as a music critic on a California newspaper at the time of the first Ban, but overnight that job was gone. I was pissed. Not at the job loss so much as the abject servility with which the Ban had been greeted by society at large. One thing though—it sure cut the wheat from the chaff. While most people just carried on, placidly absorbing whatever pap was served up on the vid-screens and radios, the real rockers turned underground.

The first pirate radio stations appeared within a month. Most were short-lived and erratic. A few people did time as a result of busts on the pirates, but in the beginning the government kept a low profile and let the country get used to it all.

A musician friend of mine dropped a word in the right place and I ended up as back-up DJ on First Clash Radio. I called myself Staggerin' Lee, because that's all I did for the first few days. We operated off a ship outside Los Angeles harbor and getting my sea legs was the first challenge I faced.

We had a good setup, as pirates went, and a long bankroll thanks to Alvin Eastingham. Alvin had inherited the remains of a pocket calculator fortune from his uncle. This was important, in that it financed the operational expenses of First Clash. But even more importantly (both for us and for him), it financed Alvin's habit.

Alvin was a record collector. He had everything from Elvis's original Sun singles to bootlegs of Polish punk groups. When you first met Alvin—or "Big Al," as he liked to be called—you figured him for a shuck. He was an overweight patrician with a misapplied spit curl and an appalling taste in clothes.

But if that was your final estimation of Alvin, then you'd missed the point. Alvin lived for the music. Unlike many collectors, it wasn't the ownership of a rarity that animated him. As he put it, "If I don't have that record, maybe nobody does. And if nobody does—then that record is obliterated from history!" I remember him standing over me, quivering. He had a nervous energy rare in such a large person. "Can't you see?" he'd say. "Every obscurity which can be brought to light only expands the universe of rock 'n' roll. It's another three minutes of rockability. And these days," he'd say, "we need every minute we can get."

How right he was.

❇ ❇

Six months after the airwaves purge came a second announcement. The government was to begin promoting the voluntary rehabilitation of social deviants. A "deviant" was declared to be "any person whose appearance, manner of speech, lifestyle, or listening habits exhibits anti-social musico-cultural orientations."

As a first step toward affirmative action, the government offered free vidscreens and computer training programs to one-time deviants relinquishing what were termed "emblems of their former allegiance." Leather jackets, amplifiers, dance posters and the like were collected and exhibited in Public Entertainment Centers across the country.

It was a time of fear and fragmentation. Records were passed hand to hand. All radios were registered—and allegedly monitored to detect listeners of pirate stations. Recording tape went off the market.

Jazz became the focus for a renewed Back to Africa movement and flourished among the floating loft societies of New York. But outside the Big Apple and a handful of northeastern ghettos, it all but ceased to be heard. There were rumors of other pockets of rebellion in the deep South—all-night dances at remote bayou roadhouses in the Cajun country and the return of the itinerant bluesmen. But to the extent that there was a national web of resistance, it focused around rock 'n' roll.

And one day, a naval gunboat positioned itself off our starboard bow and ordered us to cease and desist. Most of the equipment was confiscated and two staff members were held under arrest. Alvin and I departed hurriedly in a rented truck. In the back were 15,000 albums, 45s, and tapes . . . and precious little else.

Two months later, we were back on the air. We'd moved onto

a private ranch on the edge of the Mohave Desert and used a transmitter set up just over the Mexican border. We kept a low profile, but the word was out in the underground and we frequently found ourselves playing host to rebel rockers out from the city.

Occasionally, they'd be pressed into service cleaning up around the station, but mostly they'd just listen. Listen and talk. About why the music meant so much to them; about the strength they drew from it; about what was wrong with the world and how to right it. The usual after-hours bullshit. At least that's how I read it. But Alvin, he got taken up with it all. He'd grab me up in a big meaty hand and shout in my ear. "Stag, it's big, I tell you, it's big! Almost thirty years of solid rock and still we're outlaws. Don't you see?"

I thought I did. "Then maybe it's best we got the Bans, eh? That outlaw bit was looking pretty faded for awhile."

"Maybe. Maybe." Alvin's tongue poked its way around his cheek. "But what if . . ."

"What's that?"

"What if . . ." He fiddled nervously with his spit curl. Then he let his hand fall to his side. "Ah, forget it. I don't quite have it. What was that Dylan line? 'My existence manned by confusion boats'?"

"'Mutiny from stern to bow'?"

"That's it," he said, but he was no longer looking at me. "I've got to think about this."

Then came Blue Monday. Claiming concern over falling learning standards and rising hearing impairment, the government announced the beginning of an active campaign to *force* the rehabilitation of alleged deviants. The Under Secretary for Security droned on about "the breakdown of appropriate internal monitoring necessitating intervention by society at large," statistics were produced to show falling medians of intelligence and the American Legion volunteered their services in the search-and-destroy campaign.

I did a special show on resistance songs that night, and when I got out of the studio, Alvin was waiting for me.

"Stag," he said, "that was terrific. Especially the 'White Riot' sequence with the dub-ins from 'Riot in Cell Block #9.' You're just the man for the job."

"What job's that?"

He sat me down on the hallway bench and pulled up a folding chair beside me. "Did you ever wonder why it is we're bothering to fight off these Bans?"

"Yeah, sure. Repression must be resisted or—"

"No no no. What I mean is . . ." He pawed about like he was trying to catch and hold the very words he was saying. "What I mean is . . . well, two things really. One—why pick rock 'n' roll? Is it really that much of a danger to society?"

I opened my mouth, but he cut me off.

"And two," he said, "how come the rockers care enough to fight back? Why not just accept whatever the airwaves bring? Most people do."

"You want an answer right now?"

"No, as a matter of fact, I don't." Alvin stood up again and clumped down the hallway. Even his bovver boots didn't fit right. He turned back towards me. "Stag," he said, "we're going to do a show that gets to the heart of it all. We're going to find out what makes rock 'n' roll go."

I laughed. I mean, I had to. "It ain't as easy as all that. You got to—"

"I know what we got to do," he said with a snap. "We got to let the fans tell us. Not the musicians. Not the critics. Not even, by God, the DJs." Alvin was standing over me now, panting. "People right off the street. Insiders. Someone who can speak with insight, but from the gut."

I have to admit I was skeptical. "Couldn't we accomplish the same thing through a series of song analyses, perhaps . . . something that traces the evolution of the form?"

Alvin sat down again. He was still fidgeting. "You're missing the point," he said. "Rock 'n' roll is as much a state of mind as it is adherence to a particular form. In fact," he waved a fat finger under my nose, "individuals committed to the form could be said to embody the spirit of rock 'n' roll within themselves."

"Hmmm. Meaning, if a song plays on the radio and nobody listens—does any sound come out?"

"Exactly. Does it even exist?"

I was quiet for a moment, turning over in my mind a new thought.

"Properly handled," said Alvin, "the show should feel like an actual conversation with Rock 'n' Roll." He stood up and looked at his watch. "I got a border stop to make before morning," he said. "We'll sort this out tomorrow." I felt the weight of his hand on my shoulder. "C'mon. 'It's almost dawn and the cops are gone—let's go get Dixie fried.'"

I came into work the next day with a sore head and a nagging cough. Alvin met me at the door. I was still hesitant about the plan, but when he offered to give me his copy of The Coasters' 'Shoppin' For Clothes' if I'd MC the debate, I knew I was in.

Then came the problem of selecting participants. We had hoped to pull them from among our regular visitors, but it soon became clear that not just anybody would do. There were lots of partisans, but few who were even reasonably articulate, let alone aware of styles and traditions outside their own experience. The wily little expatriate Cockney who I'd championed had to be eliminated because he spoke almost exclusively in rhyming slang. None of the dreads could be understood without a translator. And two of our brightest hopes decided to hitchhike to Mazatlan. At length, I tired of the whole process and took a slow boat south for a bit of fresh air. Alvin assured me he'd have it sorted out by the time I returned.

A couple weeks later, I called the station from Ensenada. Alvin answered.

"Stag, that you?" Even over the phone I could tell he was excited. "Listen man, you got to get back here. You got an interview to do."

"An interview? I thought we were setting up a street level conversation on rock 'n' roll."

"Not on rock 'n' roll, with Rock 'n' Roll. And he'll be here tomorrow night."

"He . . . what? What do you mean, 'he?' I thought we were talking about rock 'n' roll."

"We were. We are." I could hear the faint wheeze in Alvin's voice that signaled rising excitement. "Remember how much trouble we had finding somebody who'd be good on the air? Well, I finally had a brainstorm. We advertised."

"So?"

"So we went on the air with a plea. On the order of 'in this time of trouble we need direction, assurance.' You know the sort of thing. And we asked, 'Where is Rock 'n' Roll? If you can tell us, come forth.'" Alvin paused for breath. "And he did."

"And he what? Al, you're not making any sense."

He sputtered into the phone. "The hell I'm not. You're not listening. This guy showed up at the ranch, I tell you. He says he's Rock 'n' Roll. Or the next best thing."

"Says he is Rock 'n' Roll. Big guy, you got a loony on your hands, not a leader."

"Stag, just get back here. I think we got some great possibilities and I don't want to debate this any further on the phone." His tone was no longer pleasant. "Or would you rather I gave 'Shoppin' For Clothes' to the new man here?"

"Alvin," I said.

"And don't call me Alvin!"

I took a deep breath. "Okay. Okay. I'll be there."

"Midnight tomorrow," he said. And he hung up.

✿ ✿

I made it back with only minutes to spare. The border checks had been unusually heavy. A special "social security" patrol had been added, which involved a private interrogation and the eventual detainment of two teenage girls for "punk-like" (that is, pastiche) clothing.

I found Alvin in the record stacks. "Hey big guy, what's happening? Hope that's The Coasters' section you're digging through."

He looked up sharply. "Hmm? Ah, uh . . . oh yeah. 'Shoppin' For Clothes.'" He was frowning. "Don't worry, you'll get it."

"You're the one who looks worried. Don't tell me Mr. Rock N. Roll ran out on you."

Alvin snorted, an unpleasant sound from the back of his throat. "No such luck." He put down the records he was holding and tried to smooth out his shirt collar. He looked at me sideways. "He's got some competition."

I just looked at him.

He held up a hand, placating. "The show's on as scheduled. But it won't be a one-on-one interview." He hesitated. "You see, that guy I mentioned on the phone . . . he wasn't the only one to turn up."

"Say what?"

"He's not the only person to lay claim to rock 'n' roll." Alvin steered me towards the studio. "Actually, it's probably for the best," he said. "More like the roundtable debate we'd originally had in mind. I'm sure you can settle the issue."

I shook off his fatherly arm-on-the-shoulder and opened the door.

There were three of them sitting around the table. And a more disparate lot I could not imagine.

To my left was a man in his early forties who sat with his chair back to front and drummed on the backrest with his fingers. He wore a lime green Edwardian frock coat that reached halfway to his knees. This was set off by a pink shirt and a string tie. Emerging from beneath the lower reaches of the coat was a pair of skintight jeans, which ended abruptly above the ankle. His feet were tapping a beat and encased in a scuffed pair of suede shoes—blue, with thickly corrugated soles.

But despite all that, it was his head that held my attention. His face was English working class: a slight thickening of the features, nose off-center and hooked as if broken once in a brawl. Along his jawline ran a scar—and a small tattoo that read RAVE ON. His hair—long, greasy locks teased back and up from his ears—swirled in a glutinous mass atop his head and fell forward in two jutting fenders over his forehead. No question at all: here was a Teddy Boy.

He smiled. The tip of his tongue was visible in a three-toothed gap just right of center. "Ullo," he said. "I'm the Raver."

I extended my hand. He did the same; and as we shook I noticed another tattoo along the back of his hand. ELVIS LIVES, it said, inscribed above an electric guitar rising up from a tombstone.

Across the table from the Raver sat a black man with a sleepy look and a half-empty pack of Kools lying in front of him. His silver sharkskin suit was set off by an inch-wide metallic grey tie that shone with iridescence in the pale studio light.

He leaned back and crossed his legs. His shoes gleamed—as shiny as a knife and almost as sharp at the tip. He wore a goatee and a slick black homburg with the brim snapped down. "I'm the Duke," he said without a smile. "The Duke of Earl." Then he half-winked and added, "But they often call me Speedoo, if you understand," and reached for a Kool.

I turned to the end of the table and the lady there took her feet back off it, cocked an eye at the Duke, and pointed a thumb at her chest. "Yeah? Well, I ain't the Queen of Hearts. My name's Sheena."

Sheena had white-blonde hair spiked out from her head with a lightning bolt of blue dyed through it. She wore full leathers that looked well worn in and a torn black t-shirt that said CLASH CITY ROCKERS. She gave me a disinterested palm slap and I watched the razor blades jingle on her earlobes.

"Well," I looked from one to the others. "Good enough. I'm Staggerin' Lee, and as you undoubtedly know, I'll be hosting this show."

Nobody looked impressed.

"We'll be on the air in just a couple minutes, so I thought I'd outline a plan of attack. We'll need to introduce you three to our listeners." I paused and considered. "Suppose we do it this way. Rather than me giving an intro, how about if you do it yourselves—just sort of run down your credentials for the audience. Give them an idea of why you think you represent rock 'n' roll. Okay?"

Sheena kicked at the table leg. The Duke's eyes watched me, soft and distant. The Raver was working on his fingernails with a switchblade, but he looked up and waved the blade in the air. "No problem, guv. That's what we're 'ere for, yeah?"

The signal flashed and we were on the air.

"Good evening, friends and foes," I began. "This is Staggerin' Lee and First Clash Radio, live and kicking . . ." I outlined the show's format briefly and then pointed a finger across the table.

The Raver leaned into his mike. "Ullo, ullo," he said. "This is the Raver, mates. Live from '55 and still on the job. You lot at the Five Crowns in Fulham 'ad better be on the glom.

"Credentials, they want 'ere. Ha. What better credentials than my very Tedness, says I, 'ey? You ask Jake the Shake or the Little Bopper if I ain't been there since the start. Why, I 'ad the first copy of 'One Hand Loose' in London. I was at the 'ammersmith riot in '58 and I saw Gene Vincent the night they made 'im climb a twenty–foot ladder to sing—gimp leg and all. I talked to Eddie Cochran three days before 'e died. I saw Jerry Lee in '63 and I fought the Mods in '64. I've been to Graceland twice—long live the King. I've worn a duck's arse quiff for twenty-five years—and I'm on my fifteenth pair of blue suede shoes."

The Raver was getting worked up. He was on his feet now, shouting at the mike. "I invented the bopper's backflip rollover with me ex-wife Madge. I seen every Wembley show since they started and I ain't yet begun to let it rock!"

In one swift motion his hand went to his pocket, emerged, and flicked his switchblade quivering into the tabletop. He wiped his mouth with the back of his hand and eyed us each in turn. "And I don't know no other kind of credentials than that, do you?"

He sat down breathing heavily.

I pointed at the Duke. He leaned back in his chair with a little half-smile and tapped down a fresh cigarette. He lit it, and when he leaned forward again he was no longer smiling. He aimed a long, bony finger at the Raver and said, "Now if you goin' go to cutting . . . why, I got a razor in my shoe."

Then he settled himself again in his chair, blew a smoke ring at the ceiling, and began to talk. "You all here talking 'bout rock 'n' roll. Shit. How's that different from rhythm 'n' blues 'cept it's a white boy plays it? You tell me.

"I grew up in Harlem. Had no . . . what you call . . . rock 'n' roll then. But we had us some music. Cats in the 'hood used to hang outside on the stoop and sing you doo-wop 'til dawn. I can still hear that high-voiced Clarence Dee singing . . ." Duke put his hand up to his ear and sang in a soft falsetto:

> Can't you find some space in your heart
> For a fool like me,
> I'm in misery . . .

Then he took a long draw on his cigarette and stared somewhere off in the distance.

"Ain't nobody had no instruments," he said. "But they could sing like nobody's business. Orioles, Ravens, Crows—all them bird groups. Man, they had them down.

"I met my first girlfriend dancing to The Drifters." He stopped and laughed. "And first time I got me a piece, she sang The Shirelles at me. 'Will you still love me tomorrow?'"

He flicked his ash and went on.

"About the time I got full grown, my brother moved over to the Motor City, and I went with. Heard me something good in Motown. But all them English groups come over and stepped on it. Diluted the dose, if you take my meaning. No offense, my man," he gestured at the Raver, "but I done heard their sound from Chuck Berry long before."

"Then came the heyday of Soul." The Duke grinned expansively and tipped his hat back. "J.B. and Otis and Aretha and the Wicked Pickett. Sam and Dave and the Tempts and—oh, what's it matter—if you don't know already it's too late now. We like to took back the charts from the white folks.

"I'll say this for the English, you folks do appreciate Soul. Why in '69, after the pot done boiled at home, I come across to England. Spent three years working Soul clubs up in the North."

"They're mad on Soul up there," put in the Raver.

"Don't I know it," said the Duke. "I never sung a lick 'til I come over and they had me lead singer!" He extended his hand palm up, and the Raver slapped it.

"Too much," said the Duke. "Then I moved to Brixton." He edged his hat back forward. "Home of cold water flats, sewer rats, and more West Indians than a calypso carnival." He eyed the Raver. "You talkin' about riots in '58, but you didn't mention the ones I heard about—Teds and Fascists against the blacks."

The Raver smoothed at his hair and looked away.

"Check that out." The Duke looked at me and nodded back in the Raver's direction. "Brixton, my man, Brixton. Like they say in the song, 'Time hard.' Best thing about it was the music. How I love that island beat. Delroy and I-Roy and U-Roy and I-don't-know-who-Roy. And that bass workout. Reggae some mean motherin' music."

He stubbed out his cigarette. "I'm telling you straight. I lived in De-troit, Philly, and both Birminghams. I seen it all. They say rock 'n' roll be for all races. I hear you. But seem to me that mean black folks inventin' and white folks collectin'."

He lit another cigarette and looked us over. "You all want

to pretend you're Rock 'n' Roll, go right ahead. But I never seen nothing as hot as James Brown at the Apollo." He turned away.

For a moment, things went quiet. I leaned into my mike to fill the dead time, but Sheena waved me off.

She stood up and shook herself. There was a faint rattle of chains from her jacket. "If you think I'm going to fall down and honor your *proud black tradition*—well, you're wrong. This for tradition." She spat heavily onto the floor. "If you know so much about English riots you'll know that punks fight alongside blacks, not against them.

"You both sound like fuckin' beadheads anyway. You claim to be Rock 'n' Roll. Shit. You're just a couple of old men gasping for breath." Her sneer was so thick it was audible. "Rock 'n' Roll's a bawling bastard. Always has been. But it took punk to cut off its balls and make it shriek.

"And you know who gets blamed for shrieking bastards. So don't jive me with who's ripping who. Women been underneath both of you since time began.

"And you tell me—where would rock 'n' roll be without women? I don't just mean without the performers—the Darlene Loves and the Aretha Franklins and the Janis Joplins. I mean the women out there that you little boys go crying about and fighting over. The ones that die in your songs like 'Last Kiss' or the ones you stick 'Under My Thumb' and discard like 'Yesterday's Papers.' I mean all the Glorias and Candys and Rosalitas that are the heart and soul of all those songs you boys swing and swagger to."

She pulled the collar of her jacket up close on her neck. "Hunh," she said. "And what about audience—what percentage of males do you suppose there were at all those infamous early Elvis shows? Who were the screamers at Beatles concerts?"

She swung around and aimed herself at the Duke. "And when you saw Mr. James Brown at the Apollo, who was it out on the dance floor shaking it down to 'Night Train' and 'Please Please Please?'

"I'm a woman and a punk rocker and proud of it. 'Cause

this time the tables will turn. We're coming up off the dance floor and taking over the mikes—and the guitars. Fight it if you want," she said. "But the new bands are no longer dick-heavy stud farms."

She stopped and looked us over. She nodded at our silence. "Enough of these phony credential raps. I thought we were here to talk about the music."

"Ah, yes," I said quickly. "Yes, indeed. Okay folks, you've heard who we're dealing with. But if we've got to hand out labels, which one would you want to call Rock 'n' Roll?" I scanned the threesome. "Speaking of which, how would you choose to describe the spirit, or the essence, of rock 'n' roll? Is such a thing possible?"

Sheena jumped right in. "Rebellion. Pure and simple. Ever since Elvis started wiggling his hips, rock 'n' roll has meant kids bucking parents—and teachers—and cops—and anybody else who tried to shove the phony adult world down our throats."

The Raver had his face screwed tight like he was thinking hard. "Could be, could be," he said. "But think of this—I'm forty-free and I'm still rockin'. I've got little tedlets of me own. Does that make me the bad guy now? I don't think so." He pointed at the tattooed words along his jaw. "See that? It don't just say RAVE, it says RAVE ON. You can't just say, 'rock 'n' roll is kids rebelling.' Rock 'n' roll is a stance you take for life. It's 'ow you comb your 'air, and the words you use—and who your mates are."

I was watching the Duke to see his reaction. He brushed one hand softly over the burnished rings he wore on the other. When he spoke, he kept his eyes on those rings.

"I'm not so sure about that," he said, in a voice so quiet we all leaned closer to hear. "Seem to me it be the music what matter. A jump-up tune for your Sat'day night strut . . . or a weeper when you feelin' blue." He twisted one of the rings back and forth in his hand. "Something real," he said. "Something that touch you deep—deep as anything." He looked up quickly. "If it can't do that, what good is it?"

"Touch you deep like what?" I asked.

A smile played at his lips, and he ran his fingertips together. "I still wake up at night, hearing Clyde McPhatter singing far off somewhere." He paused. "Damndest thing. It's always 'A Lover's Question' he be singing. Don't matter whether I got a lady beside me or not." The Duke tipped his hat back. "That Clyde McPhatter."

The Raver sighed. "Spot on," he said. "Don't make 'em like they used to."

"The hell they don't." Sheena snorted. "Don't go nostalgic on us here. Ever hear 'Alison' or 'Big Sister's Clothes' by Elvis?"

"By Elvis? You're daft," put in the Raver. "Elvis never did any such tunes."

Sheena gave a mock bow. "Pardon me," she said. "I'm talking about Elvis Costello—the only one who's still alive!"

The Raver was on his feet on the instant. "Listen you little twit," he snapped, pointing a finger that shook with rage in her direction, "I don't 'ave to take rubbish of that sort."

He made a movement toward her and I stepped between.

"Yeah! 'Beat on the Brat,'" she said.

"I mean it now," the Raver said over my shoulder.

"Be cool, woman," said the Duke. "Why you got to be that way? You all on the same side. Damn."

"Look," I interjected. "Let's try to keep our attention on the music. We're not here for you three to pursue personal vendettas . . . okay?"

We all sat down.

"Let me ask this. Let's start with the term 'rock 'n' roll' itself. How useful is that term? Can we actually agree on what it refers to?"

All three of them eyed each other.

"Come on," I said. "Duke?"

"I done already spoke my mind on that. Rhythm 'n' blues done fed the stream, but my people all the time get pushed aside when it come time to swim over to the bank."

"Financial success is bourgeois," said Sheena.

"I get your drift, mate." The Raver sucked a moment on his teeth. "But you lot are not the only ones what missed the payoff. There's as many rockabilly artists got ignored in their prime as soul singers."

The Duke looked away in disgust.

"S'true. Scores of chaps with one little record and then ignored."

The Duke cocked his eye at the Raver. "Ever hear of Frankie Lymon?"

"Course I 'ave. What about Sonny Burgess?"

"Major Lance?"

"Marvin Rainwater."

The Duke was getting perturbed. "The Falcons . . . or Johnny Ace."

"Charlie Feathers."

"O.V. Wright."

"Danny Stewart. Carl Mann." The Raver's eyes were beginning to shine.

"Joe Liggins and the Honeydrippers," parried the Duke, leaning forward in his chair.

"Jiving K. Boots." The Raver was standing.

Sheena cracked the tension. "Jiving K. Bollocks," she said. "Musty old names. How about Subway Sect or The Ratchet Boys? The man asked about rock 'n' roll—and I say you can't tie the term to history. If rock 'n' roll can't stretch to include the new, then it ain't rock 'n' roll, right?"

There was begrudging agreement from the others.

"I noticed nobody mentioned Little Eva or Shirley & Lee," she added. "Or The Bobbettes or—"

There was a sound of scuffling from the hallway and the door banged open. A boy stood there panting. His hair was wild, and he wore a denim jacket that must have been old when The Beatles played Hamburg. He carried a battered electric guitar.

"Been driving all night to get here." He gulped at his words. "Dropped the trannie fifty miles out and hitched from there." He strapped on the guitar. "Couldn't let this thing go by." He shook his head. "Talkin' about it don't get it. Don't get it at all. Before I learned to rock, I was nothing. Just another sleepwalker. Then I got me this guitar . . . and I learned how to make it talk." He punched out a riff that sounded old, yet new.

I found my foot was tapping.

"A boy and a guitar," he said. "That's what it's all about. You ask Chuck Berry."

"Ask him what, boy?" The Duke raised one eyebrow.

"Ask him why it's got to be a boy!" said Sheena.

The kid ignored the jibes. "Ask him why my name is Johnny," he said. "And why rock 'n' roll—black, white, or female—has always meant a chance for the outsider, a way out, a place to stand." He struck a ringing chord on his guitar and toyed with the intro to Springsteen's "Promised Land."

The Raver had been quiet. Now he nodded in time to the beat and said, "Kid's got a point, 'e does."

"Not on your life," scoffed Sheena. "Rock 'n' roll is about people getting together, not standing alone."

Johnny began to hum the chorus from "Only the Lonely."

Duke rubbed his palm across his set of rings. "Seem to me," he said, "we all been trying to stand alone here tonight. Sometime it got to be that way. Matter of fact, sometime I want it to be that way. Sometime you got to keep your strength all up inside yourself."

He held his fists tight to his chest and his eyes shone darkly. Johnny's guitar went silent.

"But still and all," said Duke, "if the music can't speak for a community, it can't resonate. Back and forth. You know." He waved his hands in tandem to illustrate. "I mean to say—we all outsiders, ain't we? We all on the run."

Sheena nodded vigorously. "That's it right there. We need a collective solution, not isolationist cant."

At this, the Raver hooted. "Collective?" he said. "Like skinheads, you mean? Marching in bloody rows and shouting bloody fascist slogans and bashing Pakis. That's not my solution."

"It doesn't have to be like that," said Sheena. "Skins aren't the only group movement out of rock 'n' roll."

"What you trying—" started Duke, but he stopped mid-sentence.

There was chanting from outside the studio window. It was growing louder.

Johnny broke off humming. "What's that noise?" he said.

I stepped over to the window. A bank of floodlights shone with unnatural harshness on the packed dirt parking lot. I could see a knot of figures beneath us. Boys in parkas and porkpie hats; girls in mini-skirts and chalk-white makeup, ghostly in the artificial light. Behind them came a steady stream of motorbikes arriving.

The chanting grew louder; the words more distinct.

"We are the Mods

We are the Mods

We are, we are, we are the Mods . . ."

The Raver was looking over my shoulder. "A different way," he scoffed. "There's your different way. Bloody Mods. This group thing is always the same rubbish." He turned away from the windows.

"Who says Mods are rubbish?" yelled Sheena. "Talk about Soul, why they're soul survivors." She looked to the Duke for support.

"But look there, behind them." Johnny pointed over my shoulder.

In the distance, an old school bus approached, its sides painted in outlandish colors and swirls. Half a dozen costumed figures sat waving from the roof. From somewhere inside the bus, a blaring sound system played 'Street Fighting Man.'

Duke edged his way between us and peered out at the approaching bus. He chuckled deep in his throat. "The return of the psychedelic barricade. Now who'd of thought that?" He nudged me with his elbow. "Say, maestro. Call that one if you can. Collective? Or individual?"

I went back to the table, slapped in a cassette and gave up on the rest of the show. The commotion outside was growing.

# THE WATCHER

❀ ❀ ❀ ❀

A DARK FIGURE STOOD SILENT on the hilltop, silhouetted against the cloudmassed grey. The day's chill had emptied the park of the usual strollers. Even the wind—now gusting, now flagging—seemed to move in silence.

Marlowe didn't mind. He had wanted to be alone. He sat unmoving among a clump of trees on the edge of the rolling hills and peered out at the man on the hilltop, his attention caught by the foreboding air which seemed to enshroud the figure. The man's limbs were enveloped by a sagging black overcoat. A dark beard obscured his face. His body twisted back and forth . . . back and forth . . . as if unable to settle on a course of action. He did not notice his observer.

Marlowe's leg twitched and he shifted uncomfortably against the trunk of a tree. The wind had risen and was drawing the cloudbank down around the hills. He scarcely noticed its progress; his eyes fixed on the distant figure outlined against the sky.

The man stood in the long grass and looked out over the park. The parklands rose and fell in soft green undulations. At his feet, a grassy wave descended, bearing only a few stunted trees in its downward plunge to the valley trough. In the trough, two bright red dresses fluttered above the green like butterflies. High-pitched girlish voices drifted upwards to the hilltop and settled in the dark man's ears. He watched: silent, intent. At last he turned away.

Marlowe followed the figure's gaze downwards until he too saw the little girls: bright red patches of movement in the still landscape. The dips and parries of their play left a scarlet trail of enticement lingering on the wind. When Marlowe looked back up at the hilltop, the silent spectator was moving. The figure circled slowly around the far crest and out of sight. Marlowe waited.

At length, a familiar overcoat appeared on a neighboring hillock. Again the figure paused, and seemed to shudder.

The man paced awkwardly, eyes to the ground. Above him, the sky darkened, and a low-moving black cloud began dropping rain over the sprawling grasslands. The man halted and shook off a chill.

Beneath him, the girls' chatter ceased with the change in the weather. The fluttering red dresses sought shelter amongst a nearby cluster of trees. There they paused, giggling, unaware of the eyes focused upon them.

Rain fell.

It pattered and splashed across the grasslands, but nobody moved.

Marlowe's legs had gone to sleep. There was a numbness creeping up his body, but he ignored it. The passage of time ceased to register. Stare fixed on the black-clad man, his focus shrank until he saw only the unmoving silhouette—and far below, two tiny bits of red in a dark green sea of emptiness . . .

The man moved. Knees kicking high to avoid the long grass, he stalked across the hilltop, moving now in long, awkward strides. The falling rain thickened. The wetness clung to the grass and to the legs and coat of the figure moving downwards toward the sheltering trees.

Marlowe was lightheaded and faintly sick. He felt helpless, unable to move. He watched the patch of black descending. He saw through a haze the shimmering bits of red. In the grim, grey stillness there was only the soft pattering of water striking the leaves. And the dark predator circling his prey.

Down amongst the trees, the girls waited. Their attention was held by the changing sky. They were oblivious to the movement in the encircling hills.

Paralyzed with fascination, Marlowe's eyes followed the stalker's progress. His movement through the long grass left a series of striding arcs in his wake. Slowly, deliberately, he navigated the hillside under the cover of rain.

Marlowe stared. Black . . . and red. And black drawn closer. Then closer still. Marlowe's lungs ached in their desire to scream, but still he found himself silent, staring . . .

The man moved, closer, down the hillside.

The girls huddled in silence.

A dark, hovering malevolence hung in the air. Marlowe felt now the magnetic grip of opposites drawn together in forced attraction, felt the insensate lure of the bright red dresses beneath the gloomy sky. He struggled to breathe.

The rain slackened. The wind wavered. The dark clouds rumbled and at last withdrew. The girls emerged from their shelter and scampered down the valley, their shrill voices slicing the muggy air. Dapples of red splashing up above the green.

Marlowe's breath expelled. His body sagged. He rubbed his eyes and then sought again the descending stalker. He was gone.

Marlowe jerked his gaze left and right, back and forth. There was no one. He rubbed his eyes again. Even the girls had now moved out of sight.

Yet only a moment before . . .

Marlowe pulled himself upright and stood, shakily surveying the scene. The man had disappeared. With legs trembling, Marlowe moved out from the clump of trees and stood on the edge of the hill. He twisted slowly back and forth . . . back and forth . . . in unease and growing bewilderment.

Greyness still dominated the sky. The clouds hung low and heavy. A brisk wind twisted across the hillock and Marlowe shivered. He drew his black overcoat tight around him and was suddenly afraid.

He stumbled backwards, found his feet, and fled unseeing toward the edge of the park. He ran 'til it hurt to breathe and risked a look behind him.

Black clouds hovered, brooding under evening's dark descent. Only a dim mass of hillocks still held the last obscuring light. The wind whistled over the long grass. There was no figure to be seen.

Marlowe turned again and plunged on towards the gates of the park—and the distant, welcoming lights beyond. Thoughts swirling, legs and body stiff with cold, he struggled on. His breath came loud and raspy. He fought down panic.

As he neared the gate, tiny peals of laughter burned his ears. Glancing up, he caught sight of a flash of red disappearing behind a nearby tree.

For just a moment, he turned aside. He would warn them, he told himself. But as he gathered his black overcoat in close and stepped off the path into the long grass he knew, in some deep corner of his heart, that it was not a warning that he would deliver.

Bright eyes flashed from behind the tree. A twirl of skirts, another giggle. They were there, waiting for him. Marlowe's body ached with more than the cold.

There was a welcoming squeal and bare legs high-stepping backwards through the long grass. Marlowe thought again of butterflies. Fluttering back into the depths of the park . . .

He took a step . . . and then caught himself.

At the gate he halted and shuddered deeply with the chill.

# THE DEVIL DON'T SLEEP 'TIL SUNRISE

THE DEVIL WENT DOWN TO Mississippi on a Tuesday night in June. He knew the Servant of the Lord was due in Alabama and he figured he had himself a clean shot at mischief until Wednesday noon. At the state line, he tossed a blight on the widow Edwards's truck patch, and just outside of Tupelo, he took a quick look in at the Presley woman, still growing in her belly, to make sure the twin he'd claimed was still in there kicking.

Then he cut on south and west through Okolona and Starkville, down past French Camp and McCool, riding the bottom lands and making some pretty good time. He fetched up off the Trace outside of Jackson, but being as how the legislature weren't in session, he figured all the best targets was gone. He scattered out a handful of temptations just to keep his hand in and caught the midnight special south for Crystal Springs. Time was coming due on a certain promissory note.

Now the devil had him a pint bottle of Old Crow, and what with the click-clacking of the wheels and the sweet smell of Pearl River cane, he dozed off right quick and never looked up 'til the quarter moon sliced straight across his one good eye. He let out a whoop and a beller—never did hold much with light—and when he saw the time, made a dive for the nearest window. The train kept a'rolling.

Once he'd picked himself up out the briar patch and brushed down his new purple showtime suit with the steel-grey spats and matching tie and handkerchief, the devil checked on that bottle of Old Crow. It were nigh on empty and he made it a certain thing right there. He said to hell with Crystal Springs, which was already a pretty safe bet, and set off looking for a drink. He'd fetched up alongside Highway 51 and reckoned if he walked south he'd hit a roadhouse somewhere soon.

Just outside a picked-over shack pack name of Bogue Chitto, the devil struck himself a crossroads. And setting athwart this crossroads was a tin–roofed hoe-down palace with a sign saying, "Hound Dog's. Best Beer 'til Bogalusa."

Now this set pretty well with the devil, so he tipped his South Chicago fedora down over his ear and cut on up toward the bar feeling a powerful thirst take hold of his throat. From inside the building, he could hear someone singing "Whiskey-headed Woman" and he started tapping his shoe in time as he walked.

When he got up close to the door, he saw a black boy sitting outside holding a guitar. Not playing it, but just setting there holding it like as if he was playing it. Now the devil himself was black as Gulf Coast crude and twice as sticky, but this boy outside the roadhouse wore his blackness like a shroud, pulled up all low and mean over his head.

Devil came up on the boy, eyeing him sideways and wondering where he'd seen that face, when just as he got to the doorstep, that boy looked up and stopped the devil square in his tracks. If there's one thing the devil knows, it's when somebody's got the blues. Now this boy had a look on him like somebody who not only had the blues but ate them every breakfast and twice a day for snacks. He had a blues what wrapped him round like a crawling kingsnake, tight on the neck 'til he could hardly breathe.

When the devil saw this, he backed right down the steps and put that best beer 'til Bogalusa on the back burner to simmer just a bit. This here was a potential sale. "'Low, boy," said the devil. "What's that you got there?"

"It's a git-tar," said the boy, without hardly moving his mouth. "Y'all never seen a git-tar?"

The devil edged around like he was studying on that guitar, and he said, "If it's a git-tar, why don't you play something on it?"

The boy didn't answer.

"Go on now, boy. Play me something. Let me hear you strut."

The boy strummed it once and stopped. "Can't play it," he said. "Out of tune."

"Don't let that stop you," said the devil. "Tune it on up."

"I can't."

The devil backed away and turned his good eye sideways for a better look. A raggedy piece of cloud cover slipped off the moon and the waning edge threw down a white sliver of ghost-light full on the boy's face. "If you can't play it, and you can't tune it," said the devil, "why you got hold of the thing at all?"

Inside the roadhouse they was whooping and hollering and cutting up like the devil never came to call, but outside the silence got deep as the grave itself. The boy sat looking down at his feet, scuffing his boot toe into the dirt and trying to pretend there weren't no troubling blues walking all upside his head. The devil knew better than that.

"Gimme that there git-tar a minute, boy," said the devil.

"No sir," said the boy.

"Come on now, boy. Don't be no mammy-headed mule. I just be aiming to tune it up for you."

"No sir. It's gonna stay right here by me." The boy pulled the guitar in close on his belly and sat tight.

Inside the roadhouse, a washboard started clacking, and when a heavy-mouthed singer shouted, "Mama don't allow no boogly-woogling here!" the devil started thinking right seriously about that long cold one he'd promised himself. "Boy, you as contrary as corn liquor on a deacon's breath," he said and pushed through the open door.

A few minutes later, out come the devil with a shine on his lips and a half-empty hooch bottle riding his hip. "Yo ho, boy! You still fooling with that thing?"

The boy quit his fiddling right quick and was still.

"If you ain't the damnedest thing." The devil took a long pull on his bottle. "Whatever do you suppose is the point of holding that there git-tar if you can't even tune it to start?"

The boy frowned.

"Can't sing neither, I'll warrant."

"Can too."

"Can't."

"Can. Why I can . . . I can . . ." The boy's lips triple-pumped and he blurted, "I can be the best there ever was. I can. I will."

The devil spat over his right shoulder. Twice. "What'd you say your name was, boy?"

"Name's Johnson."

"Johnson, huh? That don't mean much. You any kin to old Tommy Johnson what lives up to Crystal Springs?"

The boy's eyes came up slow and slitted. "Not so far as I know of."

"Y'all know who I mean now? Tommy Johnson?"

"Play git-tar, don't he?"

"And sings, boy. Sings real sweet. You know the whiskey-headed woman, don't you now? That one's Tommy's." The devil tilted back his head and pulled again on the bottle. When he'd wiped his lips, he leaned in close on the boy and said—real soft like he didn't want no one else to hear—"I'm the one what put him right, you hear?"

The boy's eyes shifted suddenly, straining in the dark still air. Wood smoke hung on the near horizon, ghost-drifting under the moon. The sounds from inside the roadhouse might have been miles away.

"How's that?" said the boy.

"He was a fool, boy," said the devil, and his eyes glistened red in the half-light. "A natural born delta fool. Didn't ask for nothing but whiskey. And women."

"What you mean?"

"I mean . . ." The man tipped his slouched fedora down over

his bad eye and repeated, "I mean . . . I can tune that git-tar for you. Tune it so's it never goes out again."

The boy shaped his mouth to chuckle but nothing came out.

"I can make you sing so low and dirty that the blues gonna catch the next freight train north." The big man leaned up and away. "I can send every woman in five counties to pounding at your door. Make whiskey run from your water tap."

The boy's tongue poked at his lips.

The devil was working now and he pulled himself up straight as the road to perdition, gulped once at his bottle, and tossed it aside. "How'd you like to make records, boy? Phonograph records. Make 'em so mean and evil can't nobody stand up straight when they hears them. How'd you like to whup them blues so bad that after you're dead and gone, folks gonna covet every sound you ever made like they was treasures from the tomb of King Tut? How'd you like to have white men—white men, mind you—willing to pay a thousand dollars just for a photograph of your ugly face?"

The boy looked down at his guitar and then up at the devil, backlit under the midnight moon. "Wh-what was that about the women?" he said.

"Women? Hell, yes. Easiest part of it. How many you want? Just say the word. I'll have them fighting over you like coon dogs on a kill."

The boy shook his head, slow and wobbly like a possum who can't believe he's treed. His hands left patches of sweat along the neck of the guitar.

"Why, mister?" he said. "Why me?"

"Didn't I just hear you saying you was gonna be the best there ever was? Now what no-count nigger what can't even play in a roadhouse in Bogue damn Chitto is gonna stand up in my face and talk trash like that?"

"I meant it. I did."

"Damnation, boy. I know you did. You more fool than a sow in heat." He stuck a long finger up under the boy's nose. "You got the blues so bad he walking like a man. Am I right? Now does you want to shift that load or doesn't you?"

"What I got to do?" said the boy.

The devil stretched out his hand. "All you got to do is give me that there git-tar so as I can tune it up."

"But . . . what it gonna cost me?"

The devil's face was hidden dark beneath his hat, but his voice was soft and honeyed. "Boy, if you cry about a nickel, you'll die for a dime. Don't cost nothing but your soul."

The boy jerked back. "My soul? Why . . . why you the devil!" he said. "The devil hisself."

"They ain't but the one," said the devil. He leaned up close again. "Now you tell me, boy. What good's that soul when it ain't got nothing but the blues on its back and no way to sing them off?"

The boy was trembling.

"You'll be the best, boy. Best the delta ever seen."

A cloud hung over the moon.

"You gonna whup that blues with a black cat moan. You gonna scare the angel Gabriel into blowing bad notes. You gonna walk through hellfire and ride over damnation like they was Piney Creek on a hot summer's day. You gonna be the king, boy. King of the delta blues." He held out his hand. "Now just gimme that old git-tar a minute."

The boy's hand stretched out, still trembling, and laid the guitar in the devil's arms.

The devil turned his back and worked his fingers over the strings. No sound came out. He bent down, broke the neck off the empty bottle of hooch and played the slivery shard like a knife blade sharp against the gut of the string. A low wind blew up from the south, moaning through the trees. When the devil had finished, he handed the guitar back.

The boy took it and laid it on his lap, working the edge of the bottleneck back and forth along the frets while the moaning rose in pitch.

"If you'll just sign here," said the devil, offering the cuff of his shirt. He looked at what the boy scribbled. "Johnson it is. Well, well. You're mine now, boy," said the devil, and for the first time, he smiled.

The wind gathered force in the high treetops and the cloud patches blew clear in the sky. The sharp angle of moon bit down on the devil's face, and in the sudden light the boy saw his good eye, wide and glaring and restless, as if it never slept.

"And all that other?" said the boy. "What you said about the women fighting over me. And how my photograph be worth a thousand dollars?"

"True," said the devil. "All true." And he smiled for the second time. "I'll tell you straight about the photograph. Gonna be worth a thousand easy—cause they ain't hardly gone to be none to buy. And the women? Hell boy, fighting gonna be the least of it. They gonna go for your throat."

The boy looked down at the ground, slow and frowning. "That ain't no kind of deal," he said. "I thought you was talking something different."

"No sir. That there's the long and short of it. I don't cut no other kind."

"Hellfire," said the boy. "That ain't worth my soul."

"What is?" said the devil, and he laughed so hard the boy thought it was thunder. But when the boy looked up there were no clouds at all. And no devil. Just the moon, shining lonesome through the trees.

# BY THE TEREBINTHS OF MAMRE

IT WAS HOT, AND IT had been hot already for many hours, though the sun still climbed in the sky. The heat penetrated even under the shade of the terebinths of Mamre, covering the camp like a blanket of untreated camel's hair, thick and redolent of sweat and ripening wastes. In the opening of his tent, Eliezer of Damascus sat brooding over the morning's news. It couldn't be, he thought. Surely such a thing was impossible.

Yet it was Milcah, handmaiden to the wife of Mamre himself, who had passed on the tale. She was not a woman to speak amiss, Eliezer knew, and even as he tried to convince himself otherwise, he knew that the matter was so. There had been bustling all morning long around the tent of Hagar the slave-girl and even now, as he sat fanning himself tiredly with a browning frond, two women emerged from the tent with their veils disarrayed and a ceremonial cleansing pot clutched between them.

Just yesterday, thought Eliezer with a pang, he had spoken to Eschol, the brother of Mamre, about certain arrangements for irrigation rights to be made on the passing of the master. Just yesterday it had been he, Eliezer of Damascus, who could survey the vast holdings of the camp and know that one day it would all be his own.

Sheep and cattle and asses, male and female slaves, she-asses and camels: all his. Every olive jar, every grain bin, the threshing floor and the grist mill, all wells between Morah and Shechem, the land from the river west to the hill-country of Bethel: all was to be his by right of inheritance. Now, a lifetime's dreams lay in ashes as cold as last night's fire.

The worst of it was that the master would be ecstatic, and expect the same of Eliezer. He who had slept with women for the passing of sixty harvests without siring a son . . . He who had wept often over new wine at his lack of standing among men . . . He whose wife had claimed far too much of his time and affection, considering that the woman was plainly barren and ought simply to be put aside . . . He, having seen eighty-five seasons of planting without sowing seed of his own, was now to be father of a child.

The whole camp would celebrate. Eliezer himself, as chief slave of the household, would have to oversee arrangements. He gnashed his teeth and tossed the withered palm frond into the dust. Once heir, as first child to the household born, now to be dispossessed—by a mewling, puking tot conceived by an Egyptian slave-girl of no particular repute.

He cursed the master's wife for encouraging the union. She had, it was said, brought the slave-girl to her husband herself, begging him to found a family and preserve his name. Did she realize, Eliezer wondered, that she too might well join the dispossessed?

For the course of four moons, Eliezer of Damascus brooded and waited and served. The child's mother, though nominally still a slave-girl, did such little work that the rest of the servants in the camp began to call her "Ashteroth," goddess of love, in mocking though subdued tones. It was said that she even ate her morning porridge seated, in the master's presence.

One day at the end of the season of heat, when Eliezer again sat fanning himself in the shade of the terebinths of Mamre, it chanced that the master's wife passed by. They exchanged greetings and the master's wife said, in a voice as bitter as last year's fig crop, "You do not offer thanks for the coming of the master's child?"

Eliezer bowed carefully and said, "I had no desire to offend, dear mistress."

"Yet all the camp speaks so," said the woman. "As if his mother were me, and not that Thoth-worshipping Egyptian girl."

Eliezer was taken aback by the mistress's boldness. "Does not all such praise rebound to your own credit?" he asked. "Are you not mistress of all you survey?"

The woman gathered the ends of her veil in one hand and hissed from beneath their cover, "For all the attention she pays me these days, it might be Hagar that is mistress and I the slave."

Eliezer did not know what to answer. To cover his confusion he coughed and spat a thick stream of juice into the smoldering embers of the morning fire. "To whom was the master betrothed?" he asked. "Is it not her that such slave-girls must fear and not the reverse?"

The woman sighed. "If I were to ill-treat her, the minx would run away."

Eliezer's heart gave a leap within him, and he paused in the act of spitting again. "That is a problem?" he said. "Surely that is a solution."

"Himself would be in sackcloth and ashes for the better part of a year."

"Perhaps," said Eliezer. "And perhaps not."

The woman was about to demur and pass on, but Eliezer offered her a seat of honor and clapped his hands for tea. "Good and faithful woman," he said, "I do perceive that our interests may run along the course of the same *wadi*. Might not we now reason together and encourage a rich flow of those interests?"

The moon had barely turned in its cycle the night Hagar the

slave-girl left the terebinths of Mamre. She disappeared into the wilderness of Shur, heavy with the weight of her child within her.

For three days the master wept and prayed. Then, he covered his head with a linen cloth and approached the altar he'd had built at the edge of the terebinth grove when first he'd made his encampment with Mamre. Two she-goats and a lamb were sacrificed, and all through the afternoon, the master knelt there in silence. In the evening, he returned to his tent, anointed his head with oil, and went about his business. Nothing more was said of Hagar.

Eliezer was certain that the camp had seen the last of the slave-girl and after the shock of her disappearance had run its course, he ordered himself a new tunic and made arrangements to meet again with Eshcol concerning the irrigation plans.

Then one day, just after the first of the rains had spattered the dust with the promise of new life, the slave-girl returned. She carried with her a boy-child whose name, she said, was Ishmael. The camp expected that the child would be renamed, properly, but the slave-girl claimed that an angel of her master's god had given her the name and had also saved her life by causing a spring of water to come forth in the wilderness.

Eliezer knew cant and nonsense when he heard it, but the master appeared much taken with the story and ordered a praise feast in celebration of the outcast's return. Eliezer, begrudging every measure of grain and flagon of wine, was made to handle the arrangements.

It was some days after the feast, when Eliezer had joined Mamre and his brother Eschol for a quiet game of chance under the large tree by the irrigation pool, that hope again raised its head in Eliezer's brooding breast. There had been some dispute over a contingency in the rules—settled by the opening of another gourd of Mamre's fermented grain—when Eschol leaned back against the trunk of the large tree and declaimed to the sky, "Deliver us from the ways of these foreigners, mysterious and forever bending like a wadi that does not know its own outlet!"

He said it in a tone of humor, but Eliezer, feeling still out of sorts over the reappearance of the slave-girl Hagar, said, "And what would you Amorites know of the ways of foreigners? Have you ever been to Sidon or Thebes? Why, in my father's house alone in Damascus—"

"It is not of your father's house that we speak," said Mamre, "but of your master's." He handed out the gourd to Eliezer.

"That is true," said Eschol. "One day we believe we understand his customs and religion, the next day he seems to ignore his own proscriptions. It is most confusing."

Eliezer sipped at his gourd.

"Consider," said Mamre. "Has it not always been said that your master's heir must be a child born in his house and that you, as first of those, held right of inheritance?"

"It was so," said Eliezer. "But surely even an Amorite could understand that a child of his own flesh would take precedence over simple order of birth."

Eschol, who had been busy with the gourds for hours, sat up with a spluttering laugh. "Even an Amorite!" he said. "As if we are not the owners and inheritors of the very land on which you walk? Yet you, the proud Damascan, fail to see the contradiction at hand. Is the heir to be born in your master's house or not?"

"He is," said Eliezer.

"And is it not true," put in Mamre, "that this slave-girl bore her son in the wilderness of Shur? How then can he be said to have been born in your master's house?"

The fermented grain had long since fuddled Eliezer's mind, but a sudden ray of clarity broke through his fog. It was a fine point, he knew, but on such fine points did inheritance often hinge. He set down his gourd with a splash, upsetting his pile of coins, and stared off across the empty desert beyond the camp.

Eschol belched into his sleeve and fumbled for another gourd. Eliezer, red-faced and grunting, stood up with the swift wind of insight blowing his ill-fortune westward to the sea. Hagar had nullified her bastard son's claim to title with her flight to the wilderness. No imaginary angel's calling could obviate that. Surely here was hope and justice and the wealth for which he knew he'd always been intended . . .

Like a man entranced in the dreamworld, Eliezer stepped out from under the terebinth of Mamre and let the waning rays of sunset warm his chest with their gold. He would wait, and he would serve, and when the time came for a decision, he would call by the name of the god his master claimed to serve that he, Eliezer of Damascus, was rightful heir to all the vast holdings the encampment had earned and might ever contain. Let the slave-girl rant and rave. Let those who chose deplete their livestock on the altar of the master's god in a vain attempt to influence the course of history. The real power was his, and would remain so long after the master had descended into the dark corridors of the underworld.

Eliezer slept well that night. In his dreams, pure, unblemished sheep kept jumping the stile into a fenced enclosure that seemed to stretch as far as the hill-country of Bethel.

Years passed and the master grew old and feeble. The boy Ishmael was a great trial to all in the camp, though only Eliezer dared to rebuke him. Eschol had long since agreed to the diversion of the southeastern water channels. Only time was now the enemy.

Then one day, as Eliezer was sitting at the opening of his tent, fanning himself from the heat, three men appeared and stood in front of him. Sulkily, for he had been musing with great contentment on the size of the grain silos being built in the north enclosure, Eliezer began to go through the rituals of greeting. "Sirs," he said, "do not pass by my humble self without a visit. Let me send for some water so that you may wash your feet and—"

"It is enough," said one of the men. "We seek your master."

Eliezer got up and led them across to the tent of his master. After a suitable round of greetings, he was instructed to prepare some barley cakes and a fatted calf for the visitors' repast. Eliezer passed the orders on and lingered in the shade near the master's tent, where he could admire the movements of a certain Nubian slave-girl recently acquired from the south.

As he stood there, young Ishmael came out and began to cavort with the slave-girl. Eliezer heard his master point out the boy to his visitors as his son and heir. Scarcely had Eliezer finished chuckling to himself when he heard one of the strangers say, "Son, yes. But not heir."

The master set down his drinking gourd with a thud. "Far be it from me to offend the rules of hospitality—"

"Seethe not," said the stranger. "For we mean you no harm. The boy is a fine specimen of growing manhood, but his birthright is flawed. There shall be another with a stronger claim."

"But—"

"But whatever you may say, dear sir, will not alter the matter as it stands. It is the will," said the man, "of the god who brought you here from Harran."

For a moment the master was speechless. Eliezer felt suddenly light-headed. That these strangers should pave his way for him! It was beyond his fondest dreams.

The stranger went on. "From your heir shall spring forth many nations and kings and blessings untold. Surely that is a cause to rejoice."

Eliezer, from his listening post, agreed. He turned away, lifted his hands to the heavens, and marveled at his own ingenuity in diverting the claims of that upstart Ishmael.

Behind him he could hear the stranger saying, "The very name of your heir shall be revered through all the country between the great river and the sea."

Eliezer felt his insides would burst with joy and pride. That he, Eliezer of Damascus, should be known and remembered in such a light! That someone born a slave should inherit possessions beyond count! He thought briefly of offering a sacrifice of thanks, but opted instead for a drink and set off to find Mamre and his collection of stoppered gourds.

Though he could still hear the stranger talking as he ran, the voice was gradually muffled by the overhanging terebinths of Mamre, and the last thing Eliezer heard the stranger say was, "No longer shall you be called Abram, but now, Abraham . . ."

Eliezer ran on, filled with the certitude of glory.

# BONUS TRACK: DARKTIME

✺ ✺ ✺ ✺

# DARKTIME

❀ ❀ ❀ ❀

## I

CAN DARKNESS MOVE? DOES THE web of life disappear within it, or does it coagulate, like old blood spilled out from its living source? Who rules the night?

It is not nightmares that prompt my questions. The soaked sheets, the aching head, the trembling hand on the water glass afterwards: these are common enough, and of no account to my story. It is only that when the visitations come, they come at night, even after all this time. And in the restless hours that follow, while the barque of the sun still journeys through the underworld, I wonder many things . . .

In India, there are holy men who pierce their flesh with metal spikes. There are those who can still their breath so that a mirror held to their lips is not even fogged. There are devourers of dung and living beetles and the scalded flesh of infants dead before their time.

Can those who say the dark powers are illusory convince the trance masters of Luzon? The zombies of Haiti?

When men walked in fear, bypassing the circle of tumbled stones sleeping on the Wiltshire plain, were they benighted primitives or wise beyond our understanding?

For this is how it comes:

First like a scratching in the cranium . . . then something sharp and dark and thrusting . . . a flutter of furred wings beating down through sleep and the Presence, infinitely malign, weighted on my chest . . .

The darkness is alive. I am drowning in it.

## II

It had been years since last I'd had the visitations. But there was no question what had brought them back. I'd seen Walker only the day before—or rather, the dry husk that still wore his name. He remembered me, of course. Walker remembered everything. He just couldn't do anything about it.

He'd been unlocking a bicycle from the stand outside the courthouse, and there was something in his movements—something in the way his hands wrapped up the chain—that brought back the sight of him wrapping mike cables in our roadie days. I'd hardly have known him from his face.

There was still the wide slash of mouth and, when I looked close, the v-shaped scar along his nose from the night in '69 when we'd dressed up like greasers and a pseudo-hippie in a headband and fringed jacket had punched him out with a class ring. But the glasses were crooked and taped. His whole face had widened, somehow. Thickened. And the eyes . . . no, they weren't dead. Not quite. But the light that danced in them now was nothing like the old Walker "whadda-ya-say-we-try" cunning. It was a light of uncertainty; of tremor. A light of terror.

Maybe nothing showed it better than his clothes. Walker—once the consummate Mod and always a connoisseur of style—was wearing wrinkled chinos and a dirty grey sport shirt that looked like it had been remaindered from a discount house. His shoes were patched along the sole with gaffer tape.

We did a shuffle on the pavement for a couple minutes, trading cracks about the Twins and the last live music we'd seen. "It d-don't make sense now," said Walker. "N-None of that new stuff. I think they're all possessed." He grabbed my arm, tight as death, and said, "They're here, you know. They w-walk among us." Then his hand twitched twice, like a current's jolt and his whole left side started shaking. I suggested a coffee in Artie's across the street, but he let go of my arm and said he had business to attend to. He didn't ask about Celeste.

I gave him the old handshake and watched him ride off. The bike was not one of those urban trail bikes fading jocks use for training. It was an ancient Schwinn. Missing fender, pedal brakes, basket racks on the sides. Probably a lot like the Schwinn he'd seen Santa Claus riding in the Christmas Parade in Bethlehem the year I'd seen that twitch begin. The year we met the fallen angel face to face.

I walked on in the same direction he'd ridden, past the pipestone Indian in the city hall foyer, down along the riverbank, thinking back on Walker's crazy-ass ideas. Like the time he'd wanted to use the Mississippi for a concert stage. Rent a couple of barges, strap the amp stacks tight to the deck, and let the good times roll all the way to the Delta. He'd even hustled some cash to do it—though if I remembered right, he'd used most of that cash to finance his trip to Europe. Anything had been possible then.

Above the Wabasha bridge, I stopped, looking west across the river. A splash of sun lay over the grey muddy waters of the Mississippi, still warm from the day, but up on the bridge, I'd gone cold, remembering. When I turned back towards the city, I saw Walker crossing the bridge, pedaling along on the business he'd had to attend to. Both basket racks were loaded down with newspapers. As I watched, Walker sat up straight, arm still twitching as he folded one of the papers into a long cylinder and moved off into the sunset on the far side of the bridge, ready for his delivery rounds.

Best friend I'd ever had.

### III

So if you want to start it and tell it right, where do you begin?

With Walker and the wound that never healed? Do I need to recount the parable of the rock and the sand? How about Chas? Was he a streetwise mercenary from the dark side or just another dupe? Was Ariane really the "good witch" she claimed to be or the most evil woman I'd ever known?

The choices are endless, and none more important than the one we faced that night in the Bristol flat, so many years ago. But before Bristol there was Glastonbury Tor. And before the Tor was London and further back was Spain—surely Celeste was part of all that happened. Pushed to its extreme, the web might cover all the world and for that matter, all of time. But that is absurd—and in any case, untellable. Choices must be made . . .

It started on the steps of the Roundhouse on a cool London evening in the summer of '72. The Jeff Beck Group had just finished playing its farewell gig to a sweated mass of screaming heathens and I was outside, gulping air, when down the steps came Walker, naked to the waist and bumping out the refrain to "I Ain't Superstitious."

I just stood there, grinning.

When he saw me, he gave a whoop and threw his sparkle-dot sequin shirt down in my face. "Michael, my man," he said. "You made it! Where's Celeste?"

"Still in Spain," I said.

"Still in Spain?"

"With Victor. You saw it coming. You know you did."

"Yeah, but I never figured . . . shit." He looked around out over the crowd. "Your card said meet here. That's all. I didn't realize . . ."

"Forget it," I said. "Not your problem. Hey, did that band cook, or what?"

"Like a hot plate on overload," said Walker. "But look—I mean, what is this about for you? You gonna stay in London or what?" His hair hung wet along his face. A rivulet of sweat ran down between his rib cage onto his hand-tooled belt.

"Whatever happens. I'm a free man now." I put on my company smile.

"Damn," he said. "How long were you together? Three years?"

"Four."

He was nodding already. "Of course—since Spencer's party, senior year." He looked out over the crowd again, and then swiveled back to me. "Did you hitch up?"

"Yeah. Only three days. Even had a bath in Calais."

"Not bad. Took me five. I've only been here a week or so."

"You got a place to crash?" I tossed him back his sparkly shirt and rolled up the sleeves of my own to cover the patched elbows.

"I'm kipping down in a guy's car."

"Kipping down? You sound like a native." We were on the street now, edging through the crowd flow.

Walker hung the shirt around his neck, still pivoting his head. "Name of Chas," he said, and then he punched me in the arm. "There he is now."

A black Morris Minor with a battered front fender was idling at the curb. Walker hopped in the front and motioned me towards the back seat. I swung in onto a stack of newspapers and a half-rolled sleeping bag that smelled like it had been used for cat litter.

Walker was doing introductions, shooting rapid-fire in the sideways manner that always made me think of gangsters. He had a new pair of tinted glasses with purple tones that matched his shirt. "We're going to the West Country tomorrow," he said. "Stonehenge, Glastonbury. All the psychic sites. Might even check out Ike—remember the guy I met in Delphi?"

"Gonna trip out fine," said Chas. His grin was lopsided and bent further by the drooping edges of his handlebar moustache. He wore his hair rough and slightly long; nothing like Walker's shoulder-length locks, but scruffy enough to look lived in. The whole car looked decidedly lived in.

"Come on along," said Walker. He leaned back over the seat. "Got enough mescaline for three."

"You sure that's cool with Chas?"

"Anything's cool with Chas."

"Besides," said the man himself. "Your mate here tells me you're an 'istory buff. You can give us the details, what we're seeing."

"You're the local boy," I said. "Don't you want to lead the tour?"

Chas's grin went flat. "What you mean, 'local boy'? Walker been telling you something?"

"No way. All I meant was you're English, right? Tell by your accent."

"Hey," said Chas. He turned around square in the seat. "I'm nobody, got that? Just Chas. Not from around here."

"He's on the run," said Walker.

"That's enough of that," said Chas. "We're all running from something." He pulled out into traffic.

## IV

I'D BEEN ON THE ROAD for over a year. From Sweden down across the Low Countries, out through Eastern Europe all the way to Turkey. Back across the Riviera; a stint in Morocco. Then six months in northern Spain doing a con job as an English teacher in the top private school in the province.

Celeste had been with me the whole way. We'd almost gotten married in Monte Carlo, just for the hell of saying it, but it hadn't seemed necessary at the time. Twice we'd tried to link up with Walker, doing his own tailspin in our wake, but he'd blown the rendezvous and ended up wintering in Israel. It wasn't until spring that he'd turned up on our doorstep in Barcelona, and by then, Celeste and I had begun to unravel.

Walker's presence only made it worse, though I didn't see that at the time. He and I were too tight to let anyone in between us very easily, even Celeste. What it did was make her look around. No doubt I should have expected that, because the longer we hung in Barcelona, the deeper we got in the freak scene. The Spanish counterculture was small back then. Real small. Generalissimo Franco made sure of that. Most of our friends had done time for the man, and even when they were outside they chose amigos very carefully.

Our foreignness made us safe, almost a cover at times, while the shifting relationships at the core of what was really a floating commune acted as a lure for our own experimentation. Raoul had been first, but that was a fling. No sweat, said everybody. Be cool. Be free. By the time Celeste and Victor were doing their Antony and Cleopatra act, I was on ice. Cold as stone.

Walker was ready to split. I told him I'd ride out the bacchanal, and when Celeste came back to earth, we'd meet him in London. Leave a message at Poste Restante.

Ten days later, I was hitching north through France. Tough, road-weathered . . . and alone. Still on ice.

I wanted to forget. The Roundhouse gig had seemed a good way to start. A trip in the West Country sounded even better. One stop at the 10p lockers in Victoria Station netted my travel bag and three large teas for the road.

By dawn, we were somewhere west of Hammersmith.

"You can never tell about English weather," said Chas. "Very changeable."

"Well, you can change this any time." Walker was huddled underneath an army surplus blanket, with his head tipped back against the front seat window.

Outside, the rain spilled down in sheets, obscuring the sky and the trees and even the edge of the country lane we'd backed into. I had the grand privilege of a seat to myself—barring the newspapers, of course, and two frameless backpacks, a greasy paper cone of cold chips, three warm tins of McEwan's ale, and a seedy-looking satchel with the initials "B.B." on it in gold lettering.

"No can do," said Chas. "Isn't that what you Americans say?" He tossed out another of his lopsided grins. He'd turned his dirt-brown workingman's sport coat back to front and held it wrapped around him like a barber's towel.

I shifted on the back seat and thought of the hours 'til dawn. Chas regaled us with a long, pointless story about two East Indians on holiday in Belfast, but when I asked him if he knew ferry routes across the Irish Sea, he seized up short and said to keep the bloody questions to myself. He even moved his satchel down away from my feet, but before I could react, Walker brought up the Chicago acid fest when we'd all gone down to see the Stones and he and I got to laughing for over an hour.

By the time Chas cut back in it was dark and I curled up to dream about home . . . and Celeste, somewhere south in Spain.

I woke to the sound of Chas snoring and Walker scrabbling along my foot, looking for his pack. "Up and at 'em," he said. "The spirits of the night are about to depart."

"So let them go. They did me no good." I rolled over and twisted my neck against the kinks along my spine.

"Given up that spirit stuff, have you?"

"What are you talking about?"

Walker dug out his pack. "You were the one always telling me how God was alive and well and living on the astral plane."

"So?"

"So I thought you dug that kind of thing. The mystic mood, dark spirits, signs in the heavenly realms and all."

"You're getting it confused." I pulled my legs up under me to give Walker room to work. "I was raised a believer, if that's what you mean. But just because God exists doesn't mean all that other stuff does."

"But that's the part that makes it all exciting, right? The weirdness."

"Says you."

His hand rustled in the pack. "Don't matter who. If we want to come on by sunrise we got to make a move." He pulled out a bit of tinfoil, unwrapped it, and handed out a white tab. I washed it down with the last of the McEwan's and stumbled out of the car to piss.

The rain had stopped. A heavy mist still hung in the gullies and fields, but overhead, the sky was clear. The stars made me think of Walker's shirt. The moon, which had almost set, lay above the horizon haloed by a fog that made it appear it had a twin. I felt Walker move up alongside me. His breath was moist and visible.

"We ought to hold a ceremony," he said.

"For what? Surviving the night?"

"Nah, at Stonehenge. Call up some druids. Maybe do a little time travel. Levitate or something." He unzipped his pants and steam began to rise from the ground in front of him. "If you and Chas boosted me, I bet I could get up on top of one of those stones. Like where the flat one lies across it? Get up there and dance out the demons. Too bad we missed the solstice."

The car door slammed and Chas came out, scratching at his head. "Damn cooties. Never share a squat with a Welshman, lads. Do you every time." He jogged my elbow. "Say, mate, lend us the use of your comb, eh?" He broke off and looked up at the sky. "Far frigging out. Two moons and I've not even popped a tab yet. The conjunctions must be almost right." And then, with a pause before the final syllable, he added, "Very celest-ial."

Walker looked over at me sharpish, but I pretended I'd missed the connection. Stay cold, I thought. Ice on stone.

An hour later we were inside the stone ring, circling each other like enfeebled birds of prey. My mouth was dry and bitter but the back of my head had lifted off completely and even the intermittent rain clouds couldn't spoil the mood of anticipation. We were edging into the heart of the trip . . .

## V

AFTERWARDS I RECALLED MOST THE long, wet grass, the looming face of the gatekeeper under an official hat, and the disappearing moon, hung double beyond the stones. That we'd been in the circle, I knew. That I'd touched the blue capstone; that Walker had climbed, unsuccessfully, onto the edge of one of the monoliths: this I knew too. But these were facts: as distant and unrelated as the soft thunder rolling out of the western sky. They were no part of me. At least, not then. Eventually, I would remember it all. The entire pattern of the day woven like a tapestry into my soul.

"And Chas? Wh-what do you think?" Walker said later in London, in one of the brief moments when he trusted me again and the twitching had temporarily subsided. "Was he a part of it? Planned, I mean."

"Just along for the ride," I said. Not that I knew.

"But it was too p-perfect. It fit too tight."

"They would have used anybody."

"But they didn't," said Walker. His voice was thin, almost a hiss. Like a tire losing air. "They used Chas."

An itinerant busker, on the lam from sources unnamed. Last known address: a '62 Morris Minor with peeling paint and a smell on it like something had died. Small, shabby in appearance, with a drooping handlebar moustache and a penchant for West Country ale. Answers to the name of Chas. No known talents except the ability to play jaw harp and hustle tips simultaneously. Last seen half-comatose, propped upright against a wall. Who would use him for anything?

Or was the human vehicle unimportant?

I knew only that I never wanted to see him again.

## VI

THE TOWN OF GLASTONBURY IS less than an hour by car from the ruins of Stonehenge. The same grey sky lies overhead. The same dark crows caw through the mists in the bottomlands surrounding the town. Though lesser known than the great stone circle in the Wiltshire plain, Glastonbury has no rivals for title as the oldest monastic foundation in Britain. A yearly procession commemorates its claim, drawing would-be druids and earth mothers and seekers of every stripe.

Of all the holy sites scattered about the town, none is more compelling than the Tor. It is the scarped end of a low ridge, rising from the east to something over four hundred feet—and dropping abruptly on the other three sides into the fields and osier beds that once were marshlands surrounding its island.

At the top of the ridge is a stretch of level ground. A ruined tower stands edged and solitary; visible through the country for miles around. The eye is drawn to the tower long before the town beneath it can even be seen.

The mescaline was full on our brains when we finally got out of Chas's car. From where we stood, the easy-rising eastern approach to the Tor was invisible, so we scaled the heights from the steep-pitched western side. We felt like explorers, as much of psychic as physical distances. Each labored step was symbolic. We were pilgrims progressing; climbers of a stairway to heaven.

There was still a light dew on the grass, but the pale sun of an English morning was thinning the mists that clung to the lower portions of the slope. My thighs hurt from the climb by the time we reached the upper lip of the Tor. Walker's glasses were fogged, and Chas panted like a dog on a hot afternoon. The top was suddenly flat, like a pedestal. The tower stood alone. There was silence here, a heavy silence that meant something more than the absence of noise. We stood breathing it in.

Chas must have seen her first, because he said "Hullo," in a tone of surprise. She had appeared in the doorway of the tower, as silent as the air enveloping our expanding heads. She was young and soft-featured, with blue-black hair hanging straight to her waist. Her clothes were dark: a long skirt and blouse that shrouded her limbs. She was leaning on an oversized, hand-woven broom.

"You can't get any higher," she said. The wind blew strands of hair across her eyes.

"We can't, indeed." Chas resettled the lapels of his aging suit coat. "I'm Chas. Who're you?"

"Ariane." Her hand flicked at her hair and was still. "I'm a witch."

Under most circumstances, I would ignore a statement like that. Put it down to a bad attempt at humor, or self-conceit. But standing there on the Tor, in the air that breathed around us like an invisible presence, with the morning's memories of Stonehenge and the mists that clouded the moon; standing there with the tang of psychedelics still full on my lips and watching her lean so naturally on the old broom against the cold, dark stone of the tower; just then I was not inclined to doubt.

After a moment of silence she added, "Don't worry. I'm a good witch," and slowly drew a smile across her face.

We moved closer, almost against our will, like a band of peasants in the presence of the queen. A smell clung to her—soft, but distinctive—that made me think of jasmine burning on an open fire. She was on holiday, she said, and had chosen to spend it on the Tor. At first, it sounded quite a romantic thing to do, but then I looked past her shoulder into the interior of the tower and thought about the nights: alone beneath the layers of darkness damping the sounds of the earth; moon slivers peering through the window slits; an incessantly whistling wind.

I thought I'd suppressed my shudder, but she said, "You disapprove?"

I could only shrug.

"I took you for a believer," she said.

"In what?"

"You do not know the stories?" Again the smile danced across her face, but it failed to light her eyes. "Here was the resting place of the Holy Grail," she said. "Brought here by Joseph of Arimethea. Here, too, lie Arthur, and Guinivere, and legends from many times."

"Load of rubbish, most of that," said Chas, but he moved in closer, hitching again at his coat.

"I thought they were buried on an island. Avalon, wasn't it?" My mind conjured childhood tales.

"This is the place that was called Avalon," said Ariane. "This very Tor." The wind gusted, and for a moment the scent of burning jasmine was thick inside my nose. Off my shoulder, Walker kept his silence, not looking at the inner room.

Ariane invited us in. It was cold inside, with a chill and damp that hugged at your bones like a living thing. At first I could see nothing, and felt as if I was moving under a blanket of fog. As our eyes adjusted to the light, the inner room of the tower came clear. It was empty, except for a small cloth bag resting in one corner of the dirt floor. Overhead, pale light slid through the window slits to die as it fell towards the ground. The four of us circled slowly in the tiny room. We moved constantly, as if a shift by one required adjustment by the others; as if a psychic balance needed to be maintained. Shadows moved in the upper regions of the tower, black on black, more noticeable in their absence than for any definite shape. There was a whistling in my ears.

Ariane and Chas were talking, but I was unable to understand the words. I moved closer. They traced their feet in patterns as they talked and I could see that there were lines newly scratched in the dirt of the floor. I peered in ignorance for long seconds. Then it was revealed: a Star of David set in a circle with points surrounding it. They broke off talking and looked at me, just for a moment.

"Do you ken the hexagram?" said Chas.

"Do I what?"

"It's nothing to him. He has the mark of the cross already scarring his heart." Ariane turned to me. "Unless you choose to make it so. Or your friend, perhaps."

"Walker? Not likely."

Chas poked at one edge with the toe of his boot. "Seen this used in Scotland once. Up in the Orkneys. Like a magnet for power, this. Very celest-ial." I couldn't help wondering exactly how much he knew.

"It could be a map for your journeys," Ariane went on, "should you want to return to Spain." It was not a question. What had Chas been telling her? "You know all about Spanish castle magic, don't you?" Ariane passed her broom across the Star of David, so lightly that no dust was stirred. Then she swirled it backwards and forwards in a pattern I couldn't follow and for a moment all was obliterated but a single smell. It was that of Celeste's hair, redolent with the odor of love, and we were standing together on the rampart wall of a Pyrenean castle, looking east towards Barcelona and the Mediterranean shore. A knife went through my heart, and then I was again in the tower room. When Ariane returned the broom to her side there was a movement under her skirt and I saw a flash of eyes that disappeared.

My face must have showed my confusion because Chas started giggling.

"It's only a cat," said Ariane. She spun away and an orange ball of fur uncurled from the floor. The cat was missing an ear and held its paw upright, as if in supplication. "He lives in the tower, I think. Been here since I came."

"Didn't half give you a turn, eh?" said Chas. "We must try it out on Walker."

I looked around. The light seemed to have fled from the room. Walker was gone.

Chas was still giggling.

Somewhere, I thought I heard a faucet dripping. Or was it an icicle melting onto stone?

"Walker?" I called out. "Walker, you there?"

Ariane and Chas said nothing.

I felt my way along the walls, fighting a rising panic until I emerged, blinking and shivering, into the light outside. With something of a shock I saw that during those few moments inside the tower the sun had moved well beyond its zenith. Almost two hours had passed.

The sound of a flute playing softly on the opposite side of the tower drew me like a fish on a line. A teenaged boy in a tie-dyed singlet and pyjama pants sat in the long grass playing a wooden flute. Just one breath at a time he blew, letting each note soar out of the hollow tube and into the soft, clearing air. There was pain in the notes, and hope, and a pattern that sounded medieval.

Walker lay beside him, flat on his back. From the side, only the reddish-gold tint of his hair and the upright tips of two scuffed lizard-skin boots were visible. Beyond them, at the far lip of the summit, seven cows were grazing; black and white on the green grass.

The boy blew another note and I let my spirit drift with it—away from the tower darkness, away from the damp of the earth, away from the chill that clung to my heart—up to float in the clouds.

Walker began to talk. "When I was little," he said, "I used to be afraid of dark places."

"I hear you." I was still thinking about the scene inside the tower.

"I mean really afraid." Walker's head came up briefly and then he sank back into the grass. "We had a garage where my bike was kept—clear across the yard from our house. And whenever I'd forget to put my bike away at night, my old man would make me go out alone to put it in the garage." He broke off, leaned up on one elbow, and squinted into the sun.

"I'd take a deep breath and leave the porch on the run. Down to get the bike, wheel it over to the garage, and pull as hard as I could on the sliding door. Then, while the door was in motion, I'd try to shove the bike into place—carefully, right, 'cause my dad had tools and shit all over—and hop back out before that door slammed closed." He flopped back down flat in the grass. "Always figured that some day that door would catch me and I'd end up locked inside. Total darkness. No way out." He paused, so long that I was sure he'd stopped. "Still sends me sideways, that does."

I thought I heard Chas's giggle, still coming from inside the Tower.

Walker kept on talking. Some of the stuff I knew already, but portions I'd never heard, or ever imagined I would. It was, I slowly realized, the story of his life. Not his outward life. Not a chronicle of his behavior in any physical sense, but the story of his psyche, of the hidden chambers of his heart. At times, it seemed as much a revelation to him as it was to me.

"I never asked to be treasurer." His voice was flat and bitter. "I didn't even want the job. I only came every other Sunday and that was because Mrs. Perkins next door would bring me along with her. God, I can see that pile of coins right now. Darcy Larson put me up to it. Promised me a kiss—and a ride with her on her father's hay wagon." Walker's hands moved futily in the grass, grasping nothing.

"We had a double fudge sundae each and I bought her a set of new barrettes and a charm bracelet with interlocking hearts. Probably made out of tin. Six dollars and seventy-five cents and when they found out they made me stand up in front of the entire Sunday School and apologize for being a cheat." His fist clenched tight and went slack. "Last time I ever went inside a church. And the little bitch never said a word."

I thought of my own Sunday childhood rota: the fraying, re-pressed dress shirt . . . the droning hymns . . . Alicia Barber's mini-skirt in the pew behind me . . . Bible verses repeated endlessly to the grim, corseted figures of spinsters craving control . . . and the day, distant but unforgotten, when the Holy Ghost shook me out of my practiced complacency and left the taste of fire burning on my tongue. But what did it all mean now? What difference had it made for me that Walker didn't share? Build upon the rock, we'd been told, and not upon the sinking sand. Big deal. We were still both lying in the grass of Glastonbury Tor with our brain stems strung out half the way to Mars.

But Walker had not yet shut up. "I always feel like a woman wants to trap me," he was saying. "Like I shouldn't try for anything that lasts, 'cause it would mean her being in charge. Don't you ever think that, Michael?"

I was watching the cows. Black and white on green. So simple; so right. Not cold at all.

"Still," said Walker, and I might have heard a flutter in his voice, "maybe it's better to be trapped and secure than drifting off on your own. Sometimes I think I'd almost welcome being controlled." Walker's head was sideways in the grass. His glasses reflected purple against the sky.

I was wondering why he'd chosen now to bring this up—wondering if I was to reciprocate in confession—when I felt a shadow pass across my neck and I looked behind me. Ariane stood just off my shoulder in absolute stillness. Her long robes fluttered as if her body had gone and only the wind remained. Her eyes—black with intensity, raging coals—burned their way towards Walker lying stiffly in the grass. His recitation continued.

"There's too many choices to make," he said. "Too much to decide. Half the time I get it wrong anyway."

"The choice is easy," said Ariane. "Just follow the morning star."

"I'm never up that early," said Walker. He didn't seem to mean it as a joke.

Ariane moved up closer, so that the shadow of her face fell over Walker's. "There is no need," she said. "He will come to you. He is the prince—"

"—of the powers of the air," finished Walker. The words came slowly, as if by rote. "But—" He stopped. "But how did I know—?"

"You will know many things," said Ariane, "when the time comes. You will be wise beyond your imaginings." Her voice, now, was a whisper. "When the web is sung, the called come forth."

Ariane withdrew. After a moment, Walker went on, slowly, like he was wishing he could just shut up. His words no longer connected; they made no sense, at least to me.

The grazing cows moved steadily around to our section of the hill, their movements seeming not quite random. Above us, the sky had darkened. Clouds rolled in like a fog bank, massing beyond the tower. Walker babbled on. I felt oddly lethargic, but with all the force I could muster, I sat up. "Walker," I said. "Hey man, hold up a sec." I crawled over to his side and jostled him until he responded. When he came upright, his face was white and sweating. His eyes held some private terror.

But I saw no more. A break in the clouds sent a sun shaft down onto our patch of hill and in the next instant we were all together in the grass, laid out in rows and telling tales of fantasy while the air flute blew its single notes. What had made the transition, I never knew. But now my spirit left my body and floated in softness, at rest among the clouds. I lived with God. I felt that special oneness, that unity that all people seek and die for—or die without. I knew what heaven held. I knew eternity. Perfection. Bliss.

I rolled over and looked at the cows. They stared as they munched on the grass of the Tor. Stared with big, milky cow eyes. Black and white on green. But now I saw behind those eyes the light that flickered from somewhere deep inside, and I realized that Hell, too, is real. It is soul captivity.

I slept.

In dreams, Celeste pursued me. Down a grotto, across a lake . . . her hair windswept and streaming out behind. Why did I run? Why flee the very thing I sought?

I ran through corridors towards a smoking pit, still pursued by—by what? The dying flames of love? The unreachable? Her voice was next to mine, calling in the darkness and at last I raised my hand. Celeste swooped down from her windstream ride, but even as I reached out, I saw her stop and veer away. My hand, I saw, held a bleeding cross.

Then a chasm split between us, and as it did, a heart wrench seemed to burst my chest, and now it was me who desired, but could not reach. I opened my hand to drop the cross, but it would not fall. Blood on the crosstree; blood on my hand. When I looked again at my woman-love, distant across the void, she shouted, "Choose, or separate forever. The choice is yours." And in that moment, I saw that her face was not Celeste's. It was Ariane's.

❊ ❊

When I woke, the afternoon had all but ended. Walker lay beside me, saying nothing. The whistling in my ears continued.

Stay cool. Ice on stone.

A cat meowed and in unison, we sat up. The orange ball of fur was licking at Walker's boot. The cows and the flutist had gone. Chas was sitting nearby fiddling with something in the grass. Ariane was on the far side of the level ground, dancing repeated patterns along the hillside.

The hard edge of hallucination had passed, though the taste still lingered on my tongue.

## VII

THE FIRST TIME WALKER MET Ike was at Delphi. He'd gone up alone on foot to the Oracle, hoping to avoid the midday crush of tour buses. Ike had been there already, sitting with a sketch pad on the wall of one of the outlying ruins.

They'd struck up a conversation. One of those intense, nopreliminary encounters that occur sometimes on the road and end up touching deeper than homebound friendships that last for years. Ike—or Isaac, as he wrote on the address slip—had invited Walker to look him up if he ever got to Bristol, England. Then they'd cast lots to determine the Oracle's say on the matter (Ike claiming he'd studied the process) and the stones said a future meeting was in order.

The Oracle was right, but it happened in Bethlehem, not Bristol. Quite by chance, they'd put up in the same hostel and after the inevitable backslapping, they spent two raucous nights in celebration. Their ouzo and hashish binge ended with Bethlehem's Christmas Day parade, led jointly by the Patriarch of Jerusalem's Orthodox church and Santa Claus riding a Schwinn bike. When they parted, Ike mentioned again the Bristol flat.

Six months later, Ike's offer was still outstanding.

We were out standing on the pavement of Glastonbury's high street, watching the sun sink behind the Tor and shivering slightly from the come-down. "No hippies admitted" signs were thick in the windows of the shops. Since I'd cut my hair twice for the Barcelona teaching gig, I was elected to purchase supplies. No one commented on my beard, or the hand-drawn "Resist" symbol across the thigh of my jeans, but as I passed out the doorway, a blue-haired matron sniffled into her handkerchief about "a horrible whiff of a scent."

I couldn't blame her. I smelled stale even to myself. At the car, we shared out the Mars bars and dry cheese, and under duress, Chas mentioned an old friend who lived in Devizes. The prospect of a bath and a bed—of any release, really, from the fraying nerves of psychedelic descent—set us back on the road, but thirst compelled us to stop halfway at The Goat and Compasses, a thatch-roofed pub set like a child's playhouse on a bend of the River Frome.

One round led to a second and then to a third. When Chas took a trip to the Gent's Room, I found myself telling Walker about the dream I'd had lying on the Tor. But when I hit the conclusion—Celeste turning into Ariane—he didn't laugh it off the way I'd expected. Instead, his eyes got wide behind his glasses and he shifted away from the spot we shared along the bar.

A moment later, Chas sidled back up, adjusting his lapels,

and dipped his head in between us. "Ever met royalty?" he said. "Them buggers haven't half got it made, eh? Act like we owe them a living, they do, but I reckon it's the other way round."

"Is that why you never buy your own drinks?" Walker shined his glasses on his sleeve.

Chas ignored him. "Share and share alike, I reckon. What's mine is yours and yours is mine. Only fair, inn't it?"

Walker resettled his glasses. "Yeah, but you've got nothing anybody wants."

"I'm not just a nobody busker," said Chas. His skin had gone white around his lips. "I've all sorts of contacts, I have. Friends in high places. Powerful."

"Pull the other one," said Walker.

"I know folks what can predict the future. Aye. I know ones what can speak any language you can think of—and some you can't." Chas leaned back and looked at each of us in turn. "Ones what can interpret dreams too. Been at it for years." He took a pull at his pint of beer and sucked the froth from his moustache.

"Tell him yours," said Walker. It sounded like a dare.

I shook him off.

"Got a dream?" said Chas. "Come on, then. Spill it out."

I passed again. "It's my business," I said. "Nobody else's."

"Piss on your poxy little dream, anyway. I've got contacts. Friends in high places."

Walker watched me steadily for a long moment and then raised his glass for the publican to see. "We'll have another round on that," he said.

And we did. It wasn't the last.

Our reception, hours later in Devizes, was, as a consequence, less fulsome than Chas had led us to believe was due. We were allowed to pass the night on an attic floor and given eggs and toast in the morning by a tight-lipped woman with back-teased hair and arms so pale they'd have made an albino look robust.

As we were packing up, her husband took me aside and said, "How do you know Bu—I mean, Chas? Do you dabble as well?"

"Dabble? In what?"

"The dark arts, surely." The man looked back over his shoulder, and then again at me. "Has he never spoken of it to you?"

"I'm not sure. He's hinted at this and that, but—"

"But you never know with him, do you?" He held his face close to mine for a minute, as if he was searching for something. "That boy'd hustle his granny if he could. Is that your game?"

"I think you've got us wrong."

He pushed a rolled-up five pound note into my shirt pocket. "It don't matter either way," he said. "Just see you don't come back, right?"

We were out the door by mid-morning, still edgy from the day before and open for a change in plans. Walker had put on a crushed-velour shirt with multi-striped trousers, a pocket watch chain, and a gypsy bandana bound at the neck. His hair was pulled back in a ponytail. "We could always do the rest of the mescaline," he said. His grin was a flash of white.

"Don't be daft." Chas pulled the lapels on his coat up tight around his neck. "We'd do ourselves a damage." His fingernails, even after our cadged baths, were dirty and chipped.

"I know a guy in Scotland," I said. "If you think the car would make it."

Chas looked sour. "I'm not keen on heading north. Had a spot of trouble that way before."

"How 'bout Bristol?" said Walker. He moved into a frozen dance pose. "'Kids in Bristol are sharp as a pistol, when they do the Bristol Stomp!'"

"Sounds good to me."

"You got an address?" said Chas. "Some good pubs in Bristol."

"Cat I met in Delphi. Let me see here." He dug into his pack and came out with a little black book.

## VIII

IKE ACTED NOT IN THE least surprised to see us. "Been expecting you," he said to Walker. "Just wasn't sure when." He gave me a handshake and a backslap, but when he turned to

Chas, he said, "Seen you before, haven't I?" and barely extended his hand.

"Not likely, guv," said Chas. "I rarely come west of London."

Once we were inside, Ike chucked our bags behind the door. "Tea? A joint? Three packets of Smarties? What'll it be?"

Chas spread himself out on an oversized pillow on the floor. "Ooh, this ain't half bad," he said. His jacket was already off and his feet were propped on a stool. "Feel a bit of a pasha, being waited on and all."

"Don't get yourself too settled, boyo. Your turn will come." Ike's smile was quick, and just as quickly gone. From the kitchen he called out, "Up for some company?"

Walker looked at me. I shrugged. "Sure," he yelled back. "Especially if they're ladies."

"Oh, there'll be ladies all right." Ike came back into the room carrying an enormous brass tray loaded with cups, a sloshing pot, and an engraved tobacco tin with an oriental design. He tucked stray wisps of black hair back behind his ears and started licking cigarette papers together while we waited for the tea to brew.

## IX

It was Walker who'd first introduced me to Celeste. Back in high school. I'd known him at the start as the slickest white mover on the dance floor at weekend rave-ups. Always groovin', rarely alone. I'd stroll into Danceland of an evening, or Mr. Lucky's, or The Barn, and inevitably, there'd be Walker, shaking it down with some northside filly in hip-huggers. We started out talking music together—Brit Invasion, Soul, Dylan—and the further we went, the more we found in common. Not only did we dig the same sounds, but our moments of manic inspiration seemed to coincide as well.

Whenever we did get together, I knew that before the night was through, I'd be traipsing off on some fool-ass adventure concocted by Walker's overload of creative impulse.

It might be crashing a barn dance on a mutilated grain combine, or throwing eggs at cop cars from the bridge over the Interstate. It almost didn't matter what we did, we'd tear ourselves up laughing so hard. Once, a bunch of us infiltrated a regional Young Republicans convention, passing ourselves off as delegates from Chicago, and managed to splinter the Human Rights caucus by running Walker as the Anti-Normal candidate. Then we hijacked the booze supply and holed up behind locked doors in one of the rooms until the convention chairman begged for mercy and we agreed to split. Came out dressed like Arabs in sheets and towels and demanded safe transport to the border.

Whatever he did, Walker did it with style. Panache. The way things looked were a whole big deal to him. He was a Mod even then. Almost the only one in town for awhile, because the styles were so hard to come by. He'd make his own clothes if he had to: sew on epaulets or widen the bell around the cuff of his pants. Once, he took a white dress shirt and spent three weeks straight hand-designing paisley patterns from neck to tail.

No way would I have had the patience for that, let alone the desire. There were times when I wondered about Walker's obsession with the surface of things. To me, it was what was underneath that mattered. The non-ephemeral; the unchanging.

Walker always gave me crap about my "mystic tendencies," but I thought he was missing the point. Maybe it was the after-effects of those weekly childhood marches to Sunday School, or some deep-seated need for cosmic order in my life, but there was no doubt in my mind that a divine being was watching over us all. Exactly how that worked, or whether all religions had access to that same divinity, I couldn't have said. I was big on the ineffable.

That didn't mean I bought into the details of any organized religion. Rules and regulations were not for me. And when people talked about saints, or angels, or demons of the night, I scoffed at their pathetic anthropomorphism. I was hipper than that. I was free.

So was Walker, and when he said there was a girl I ought to meet, I took him at his word. Celeste DuBrey had eyes the color of abalone and a tan like a Polynesian surfer. She wore her hair shorter than mine—a razor-cut Carnaby Street 'do that always made me want to nuzzle her neckline. She laughed a lot, shouted when she felt like it, and never once backed off a dare. Pretty soon we were a threesome, fleshed out periodically by Walker's lady-of-the-day, but always tight between ourselves. Always that feeling of being on the edge of something big.

I thought I knew her pretty well, but the real surprise came when first we hit the road together. Just the two of us. Celeste shed her American skin like a butterfly molting. It wasn't just the change in daily patterns: the morning espressos, the castle walks, the long, lingering evenings in canal villages or Turkish ruins. It was a whole new sense of herself; of who she could be. Her clothes changed from jeans to full-length, flowing skirts. Her hair grew long and was wound up over her head in plaits and braids. She learned bits of French and Italian, and began asking questions about architectural styles that left me baffled. Now when we met locals in a *taverna*, or other travelers along the road, it was Celeste who struck up the conversations and found ways to make our idleness idyllic.

But Walker never saw any of that. He wasn't around. And when he did turn up—the fires of charisma still flaming in his eyes—it was to the old habits that he and I returned. Habits Celeste had left behind. We slid back onto the treadmill of American freak-style with an ease that should have shocked us, as if we'd forgotten all that we'd learned on the road abroad. So as Walker's flame burned hot, Celeste's butterfly rode the air currents out away from the heat. By the time I'd sussed the drift, Victor was already tracing her wings and staying cool seemed the only option I had left. I was entering the Deep Freeze.

But I never quit thinking on Celeste. And all the unanswered letters I sent winging south to Spain kept the message clear: there was still a chance to return.

## X

THEY CAME IN STRAGGLES THROUGHOUT the early part of the evening. A pair of university students, Chris and Derek, in blunt-cut hair and ragged jeans. A tall, gaunt woman named Hilary whose left eye fluttered and whose attention, throughout the night, was taken up with her cat, an orange tom with one ear who alternately hissed and hid on the landing. There was a quiet couple from Bath whose names I never did get. They ran a health food shop in the basement of a Georgian town house and talked only of grow-lights and the miracles of indoor planting techniques.

Then there was Maggie. She'd come in behind a couple of the others and sank instantly into the space between sofa and wall, so that it was several minutes before I noticed her at all. She was plump—or rather, she had been plump, and still retained a general bodily outline of roundness. But the skin on her upper arms sagged. Her face looked drawn and pale, as much as could be seen beneath the thick sheaf of hair that hung down around her eyebrows. Stiff, straw-colored; it might have been a hedge that a tired face peered through. Maggie wore a dun-colored sheath dress that hung to her ankles. She was barefoot and silent for hours.

Ike kept busy with the tobacco tin. Derek—or maybe it was Chris—manned the turntable, spooning out helpings of the Floyd, a Dutch metal band called Supersister, and the folk singing of a local boy they knew called Keith Christmas, whom Ike claimed was a warlock. By the time the third joint had passed, I'd curled up on one end of the couch, content to ride the smoke cloud for the duration.

Chas was in his element. He played the jaw harp, recited dirty limericks, performed a disappearing coin trick with a 50p piece (nobody seemed to care that it never reappeared), and with Walker chipping in here and there, embellished on the previous day's events with a grandiosity that made me proud to have taken part.

At the outset, Walker was fairly subdued. But Maggie seemed to touch a chord with him, and twice in the early evening I saw him hunker down next to her on the floor and try out his charm. Walker was never rapacious. His scene was not a simple seduction, but more a combination of desire, circumstance, and a genuine feeling of concern for someone on the outskirts. "Great ankle bracelet," I heard him say, and "Any good dance halls in Bristol?" Her replies were inaudible.

The health food couple was serving out cups of chamomile tea when a buzz ran through the room. I looked up from studying the Supersister album to see Ike tapping pills out of a canister.

"Everybody in on this?" he said, looking around the room.

Walker turned away from Maggie. "What's up?"

"Purple micro-dot," said Ike. The grin flashed and was gone.

"Super stuff," said one of the university lads.

"Absolutely ace," said the other. They each reached forward for a tab.

Chas, still sprawling on his oversized pillow, yawned once and extended his hand. "Why the bloody hell not?" he said. He rolled the tiny pill across his fingertips as if it might heal and cleanse the chipped, dirty nails. Then he popped it in his mouth, swigged at his tea, and leaned his head against the wall with a final twitch of his drooping moustache.

"Walker?" said Ike, extending the open canister. "Grab one for your mate as well."

Walker hesitated and I waved it off. "We're still a bit loopy from yesterday," I said. "Not quite back to earth."

"That's the whole idea." The gaunt woman, quiet for so long, was looking up at us with an unusual intensity. Around us, people were gulping and draining their tea. Derek moved over to the turntable.

"Let me take a leak first," said Walker, and when he saw my look, he added, "just to think it over."

I followed him down the hall. When he came back out of the can, I was waiting. "You honestly telling me you're ripe for a crowd-scene acid trip after yesterday?"

"You ever had purple micro-dot?"

"That's what I'm afraid of," I said. "If those are two-way tabs we'll be in never-never land 'til morning."

"Yeah, but shoot. It looks rude if we don't go along."

"Rude? What is this, Emily Post's rules of etiquette? We just tell them we're fried."

Walker rubbed his hand across his chin. "I do feel pretty worn down. I keep thinking about that Ariane."

"So think about Maggie instead. How hard is that?"

Walker's eyes flickered. He looked past my shoulder, down the hall. "There's something about her," he said. "Almost reminds me of myself."

"Maggie?"

"She seems so fragile, somehow." Walker's hand flexed in the air and went limp.

"All the better you should keep your head together and ease her through the trip. Look—" My hand tapped his chest. "It's not like we're hurting for a high. There's plenty of smoke, probably more lager—"

"Okay, okay. Deal," said Walker. "No trip."

We headed back towards the laughter in the living room.

Ike listened to our disclaimers, shrugged once, and reappeared a moment later with two glasses of wine. "To ease the withdrawal," he said. "Don't worry about the sediment. It's just a bit of cork."

Walker drained his glass and moved over to sit by Maggie. I took a long, slow sip and then another. Maybe it would quiet my nerves.

Silver petals slicing sideways. A neon hum from the fish aquarium in the corner and two green eyes framed by padded paws peering through the sides. On the floor the carpet patterns spin and whirl. Their kaleidoscope is the precise equivalent of the conversation drone that hovers in the room.

My mouth, again, is bitter. My body jelly, conformed and useless on the couch. The wine, I think dimly. They must have dosed the wine. But now it hardly matters. Across from me, Chas—glassy-eyed and somnolent—chews on the ends of his huge moustache.

Somewhere I hear a faucet dripping.

## XI

CELESTE STOOD IN THE DRY channel of the aqueduct, dropping stones onto the weeds that choked its base. Plop, plop, plop. Like a faucet dripping. In the far distance the Mediterranean shimmered, but here, among the Roman ruins inland, the dust lay dry and undisturbed.

I sat in the shade of an outlying wall with Raoul, Pepe, and Dolores. The day was hot and enervating. When I licked at my lips they were salty with sweat. The others were watching the progress of a colony of ants, urging them on with mock fervor and Catalan oaths. We'd all been tripping since sunrise.

Victor had brought the doses back from New York. Victor, grandson of Catalonia's poet laureate. Victor, smooth and suave and only slightly tinged with the olive tan of Mediterranean blood. Victor, former leader of the banned Communist Party youth wing and now the unofficial head of Barcelona's underground. We'd talked life and love and political theory together often enough, but his interest, until today, had always seemed professional.

Had something in New York changed him? Or was it just the acid helping me to make connections I hadn't caught before? He'd hung close to Celeste all morning. Montserrat, his girlfriend, was off visiting her brother in jail. But that was nothing new. What was new was the invisible polarity I could feel between him and Celeste.

Beside me, Pepe was shouting, "*Ostia*" and slapping at his ankles. Up on the aqueduct, Celeste shaded her eyes, looking down at our puddle of shade. The long, flowered skirt blew taut across her thighs. Then a shadow obscured one side of her face. It was Victor, leaning casually over the side of the aqueduct himself. Taking her arm and saying something. Laughing, pointing; holding her close.

I could hear nothing. In fact, from where I sat, I could hardly see that he touched her. But I knew that something had passed between them. Something that I would never recover for my own. I stirred in my place and spat sideways onto the ground. But the bitterness on my tongue remained.

## XII

AN HOUR PASSES. MAYBE MORE. Ike has given me a picture book to look at. It is an elegant, full-color series of Botticelli prints, rendered almost luminous in the soft arc of the reading lamp. He has handed it to me open at a certain page and doesn't withdraw. He stands to one side, his upper head beyond the cast of light so that only his mouth and the line of his chin are visible.

I am numb.

Side by side, the open pages show me two prints rendered five hundred years before, but as alive and fresh in my hands as if the paint had not yet dried. There is the full-length figure of a young woman wrapped in Renaissance robes and moving towards the viewer. Her face looks familiar, but it is not until I read the picture's title that my brain begins to fog. *The Return of Celeste*, it says. Even her hair style mimics my remembrance.

Is it a sign? I wonder. I've been thinking of Celeste, certainly, but I haven't mentioned her name to anyone except Walker in days. And then, on the facing page, I see an angel, wings unfolded, reading from a scroll. His back is to the lovely figure in the Renaissance robes and the title beneath his burning feet is simply, *The Archangel Michael*.

Stay cool, I should tell myself. Don't let him know. But by the time I look up at the Cheshire smile above me—face still blacked above the light, smile hung like a gallows' noose—the deep chill inside my heart cavity has spread outwards through my limbs.

❂ ❂

"I'm not coming with you," she said. "Today was the end."

"Look, we'll forget hitching. We'll take a train. A plane. Anything."

"It's not just hitching, Michael. It's . . ." She shook her head and moved away, turning to look out at the street below. It was a view I knew well. The peeling facade of the apartments across the way, the *pharmacia* sign creaking in the breeze, the tired bus stop figures leaning on the cut stone wall. Just now, I didn't want to see it or any other part of Spain. I'd had it. All I wanted was a clear road north—and my woman beside me.

"So what is it then, really?" A bit tired; a bit pissed. A whole lot bewildered.

"It's everything," she said, whispering behind her hair.

"It can't be everything." I moved up to where she stood at the window, hoping to influence her by sheer proximity, but she shook me off.

"It's too much . . . you," she said at last. "Too much Michael. I don't want any more."

"Too much Michael? What the hell is that supposed to mean?"

She whirled on me. "You're so full of yourself, aren't you? Why would 'Michael' ever be a problem? Michael, the almighty!" She pushed past me to the inner door. "You're not half as important as you think you are."

The door slam seemed to echo for a long time. Or maybe it was her words. "Michael the almighty." It was a phrase I'd heard before. A biblical one. Michael was the archangel of the Lord. Michael had disputed with Satan himself. I'd had my name used against me plenty of times growing up, especially when I got in trouble at church. This felt different.

The whole scene felt different. From the upper window, I

watched the street, and soon Celeste appeared, half-running. I followed her progress until she was out of sight. There was no telling when I'd get to see her again.

## XIII

It feels as if weeks have passed since last I looked around the room. Bodies recline in various poses. Chas, on his pillow throne, is playing the jaw harp silently. Maggie is still squeezed into her tiny spot along the floor—Walker no longer at her side—but I have no more than registered the fixed, unfocused look on Maggie's face than I follow her line of vision to see a woman seated at the axis of the room.

I have never seen her before, but somehow I know she is a witch. Is it because of the way the others have grouped themselves around her, tense with anticipation? Is it the smell—of jasmine burning on an open fire—that seems to hover in the room? She is wearing an embroidered red dress with tiny mirrors fixed along the sleeves and bodice. Her hair—hennaed in the European style—should clash disturbingly with the dress, but it is not her hair that holds me. It is her arms. They move and twist and writhe, snake-like, in circled patterns about her head. At first it seems she is mimicking the musical lines of the Keith Christmas album someone has placed again on the music box. Keith, with his warlock chants. But then I sense an inversion: that it is the music and the carpet patterns that conform to her moving hands. The patterns remain visible in the air long after being sketched, just as the eye retains retina impulses even after the lids are shut.

A web is being woven. It is a spoken web as well, laid like a chant above the song, but unintelligible for the time being. I am unable to look away.

For a long moment I see this woman's face—framed by red, by flashing mirror—across from me on a canopied bed. Her arms still moving; entwining, seducing, luring. I want to stand up and give myself to her there on the floor, but the ice inside my chest weights me like a stone. There is a whistling in my ears and a crawling sensation at the base of my spine. With an effort, I look around for Walker.

He is almost beside me, upright in a chair, but when I speak his name there is no response. His head is thrown back on the chair's broad curve—hair splayed out like an aboriginal doily—and he is looking, not at me, but at the lady in red. His stare is catatonic.

❊ ❊

Snatches of songs flit past. A tape reel fast-forwarded through the ozone, playing Blind Faith's "Wasted and I can't find my way home," on into the Dead with "Trouble ahead, the lady in red," and the Stones chanting "It's so very lonely, you're two thousand light years from home . . ." Pink Floyd crashes out the power chords to "Interstellar Overdrive" and slides into the hypnotic swell of the guitar-washed "Meddle" suite.

Is any of this alive outside my brain?

My chest is weighted with the sins of all the world. In desperation—Out, I think. Get out. Air, you need air—I jog Walker's elbow and he whispers, "I have no control." Looks past me, vacant. "I'm angry, but I've lost control." No one else in the room seems to have noticed anything unusual at all.

It takes every fiber of concentration my body can bring to bear, but I manage to pull myself upright. Walker, still half-catatonic, responds to my hand. When we are both standing, I mumble something about needing fresh air. The room is spinning, not wildly, but within the patterned web of the mirrored sorceress beside us.

Ike points us to a door. "Up on the roof," he says, and the Drifters' reference gives me strength to turn the handle. Inside . . . a room. Tiny, pitch-dark. A set of stairs just visible, like a stepped pyramid, and upwards a trap door. Our passage to the roof. Behind us, the door to the living room swings shut and the blackness is complete. Walker stumbles against the steps and lunges for my arm. I try to shake him off, fumbling for a latch. The trap door is bolted and sealed. Now the metallic taste in my mouth leads down to a throat choked with pain, as if I'd swallowed a knife. Walker's grip on my arm could be a vise. I beat feebly on the locked trap door, but already I know there is no escape.

We back away from the trap door, stumbling together, and as we turn, the edges of the room begin to swim slowly into view. There is padding on the walls and pairs of metal circles set in place, neck high, at the corners. The walls seem to pulsate with a living beat—coming closer, then retreating, coming closer again.

Walker moans into my sleeve and pulls me with him, wildly, as if he can no longer find the door, 'til we slide across a too-slick floor to fetch up against a solid wooden object, covered with a cloth, that looks like nothing so much as an altar, but an altar designed in parody of anything I've ever seen before. A stench of decay hangs over it. Something whose smell sends me back into my past: back to the body of the widow Bartlett laid out on the bed next door and us kids peeking, then running away, running 'til our sides ache and our breath comes quick and sharp and frightened.

In the locked upper room now, I squeeze my eyes tight, willing the scene away, but the stench refuses to die.

Walker's gasps are audible. Try as I might, I can't remember how to call for help. I keep my eyes shut tight. Web patterns still dance at the edges of my eyeballs, but now . . . in the complete and awful blackness . . . something living is beginning to pick at my brain . . .

The first flutters of invasion are exploratory. Later they will become excruciating, but now they are deft, subtle, almost massaging. A bending of the will rather than a frontal assault. Then she is there: the soft interior of a canopied bed beckons, body under the sheet warm and welcoming. No mirrors now. No red embroidered dress. Just the tangled lure of arms and legs and tentacled hair.

Why not lie down? The thought shapes itself inside my head. Taste this, feel that. Relax against the skin. Outside is cold and distant. Why not lie down? Here is the protection you truly desire. The self you wish to become. No decisions are necessary. Acquiesance is all.

A face floats up, disembodied. It is not that of the lady in red anymore. It is Ariane.

"Choose," she says, and the words echo somewhere inside my heart. "Choose the prince, for he is here. He walks among us."

I mumble; what, I do not know.

Her eyes burn like raging coals. "It is power," she says. "And knowledge. Choose, and you will become like God."

"Never," I say. "Not a hope."

"How do you know until you try?" The voice is soft with caress.

The answer comes despite me. "No one can."

"I know many who have."

Then her face dissolves, and beside me, Walker whimpers. "The prince," he breathes, and again we stumble backwards.

Tiny wings beat against my cranium. There is sudden pain.

Another voice—the lady in red. *Think of these as angel wings. Your very own. And our minds as twins, to share the earth . . . Think of all your long desires, embraced inside our bonds.*

*Come, enter the tower of night. It is not dark to those who live there . . .*

A snake is crawling up my spine.

When we staggered back into the body stew of the living room, everybody's mouths went tight. For a moment, I thought they were surprised to see us. The woman at the axis of the room never turned, never moved, but mirror flashes ringed us like shooting stars and her arms, as ever, writhed on. My eyes hurt from the inside out.

"Out," I said. "We need to get out. A bit of air."

"You didn't like the roof?" said Ike, but I could no longer answer. Walker clung to my arm like a leech to a wound.

Chas was helping himself to another cup of tea. His eyes hung heavy-lidded as he poured. In her corner, Maggie began to whimper.

I knew I couldn't possibly navigate my way through the tangle of bodies to where an open door waited on the far side of the room. I wanted badly to lie down. The base of my spine was numb and twisting.

Then the lady in red was facing us—alone, it seemed, with the others frozen in postures like porcelain figures who'd been collected long ago.

*Come, enter the tower of night,* came the voice that did not speak so much as it breathed, and simply was. *The dark angel beckons,* it said . . . *he will not be denied.*

A dank chill clutched at my heart as if it were a well, musty from disuse. In front of me, the lady in red passed her hands across her face and held them still. Then the floodgates opened and I was drowning, upright.

I screamed through my gurgles (though it must have been silent, for no one in the room moved at all) and as the inrushing tide swept me under, I shouted the name of a God who once had hung on a tree; who'd claimed to have died for me. Thunderclaps knocked me backwards and a light shaft plunged the well inside me, emptying the pain like water poured from a gourd. I felt whisked clean. Dry. Remade.

My feet moved forward, and behind me, Walker lurched along in my wake. At the far doorway the cat screeched and darted past us onto the steps leading down to the street. The bowl she'd been drinking from spun briefly and wobbled to a halt. We stepped over the spillage, easing past the spreading pool of redness, and made a dive for the door.

The cat hissed as we passed, but at the foot of the stoop outside we sat down, exhausted and breathing like divers coming up for air. The night air hung a damp cloak over our backs and looking down, I realized we were barefoot.

Walker's feet were smeared with blood but when I pointed

it out, he made no mention of pain. We could find no visible cuts. Just as I started wondering about that drinking bowl the cat had left, there was a rustle at the top of the stairs. When I looked up, the cat had disappeared. Ike stood in the doorway, grinning his Cheshire smile.

The music inside the flat could no longer be heard. Whatever lift of energy had carried me across the room seemed to have dissipated as quickly as it had come. I felt weak again, and violated—as if that hanging tree held me too. I could scarcely remember the Name I'd shouted aloud. There was a slink of fur along my leg and the cat ran down the street.

## XIV

THROUGH THE SILENCE OF THE Bristol night, we walked. Our feet padded in time, like lonesome soldiers, over cobblestone, over concrete, over flagged intersection and grass-edged boulevard. Around us, the city slept. But always—and even the slightest glance at Walker confirmed that for him it was the same—a dark presence still beat at the windows of my brain. I felt I was fighting for my life and that, for the first time, my foes were both inside and out. Wisps of smoke obscured my vision, pressing inward like hints of a fire to come.

I was filled with inner loathing. With panic. With the horrible truth that I was a fallen being incapable of resisting the heart of all darkness. I knew only to walk; to move. Further and further away from the web pattern of soul capture that inhabited Ike's upper-storey flat.

Street by street, we walked, silent. I no longer thought. I only prayed—and now, unable even to shape words, I let the rhythm of my slapping feet beat itself into wordless prayer, flung upwards in vain desperation.

It was the darkest hour I had ever known.

❁ ❁

They'd told me of Satan, of course, before I'd even started school. Painted him clearly enough: the horned figure; the forked tail. The old serpent who was the tempter of all mankind. He was hardly the staple of Sunday morning lessons, but his presence was always there, hovering at the edge of fear.

But I'd left that all behind with childhood. Laughed at allusions to the fallen angel, or warnings about Lucifer's pride. These were for the ignorant, the unenlightened. Surely nobody with reason still clung to such a simplistically dualistic sense of the world. When Ariane first said, "Choose," remote inside the Tor, I'd scarcely understood the terms she offered.

Now, a day later, I found myself a barefoot penitent, begging for that power of choice.

At last, on a hill above the city, we stopped. The street arched its way across the mound of the hill, contained by a set stone wall. Beneath us, subdued by midnight, the giant city slept. Houses, shops, factories, playgrounds. The great noisome collection of human needs and desires slumbered under the cold edge of night.

We leaned on the wall. Neither of us spoke at first. From somewhere inside me (or was it out?) I felt a faint twinge of solace. A pinprick of illumination, then warmth, steady and certain. A counterforce to the dark, beating wings that still clawed at the edges of my mindscape.

Walker—open-mouthed beside me—looked up suddenly and said, "You're an angel."

"No, I'm not." How well I knew.

"Get away," he said. "You're shining." He moved down the wall. "You're Michael, the angel. Like in the book."

"No, I'm not."

"You're behind it all. You're doing it. Get away from me." Walker was crouching as he retreated. "Make it stop."

In the distance, a train whistled and we both turned at the sound. Tendrils of fog were drifting up from the rooftops, but the city slept on beneath us. The train whistled again, closer this time, with the dim chugging of engines a drumbeat under the shriek.

Then it was in view, winding out from the battered Victorian core of Bristol in a slow, sinuous curl. Huge, grey-black, and throbbing. On it came, bending and twisting through the row-housed streets below until it stretched from horizon to horizon. I was numb along my spine because the same serpent-tongue I'd felt licking up my backbone lay snaked out across the entire darkened city: a living thing—no metal pullman cars at all, but anaconda skin slithered over the tracks.

Before I could speak, Walker said, "It's a snake," and the rasp in his voice abraded my heart.

"I see it," I said.

"If you're an angel, stop it!"

I started to say again, "I'm no angel," but when I turned toward Walker I stopped. He hung on the wall like it was a life-ring, limp and feverish. Even in the moonlight I could see the sweat lines running past his ears.

"Stop it!" he said again, but I was silent.

The snake-train whistled once more, mocking us, and wound on out from the city's heart towards other towns and cities that slumbered through the nighttime, unknowing.

My chest was huge with grief. Fog hung all around us now, cold and obscuring, and we each clung to our spot along the wall. The wings beat inside my head. Somewhere through the smoke clouds I sensed a light source, but before I could react, I heard footsteps echoing up in the wake of the disappearing train.

Looking around, ever so slightly, I saw a dim, covered figure climbing the curve of hill we'd walked just moments before.

Closer came the hovering wings. Furred and beating. Soft claws pried at the edges of my consciousness. Beside me, I heard Walker gasping, but now I was unable even to turn my head.

The footsteps came on, rhythm-stepped to the fading sound tunnel of the snaking train. An endless line of footsteps, like eternity itself. Walker gasped again, and retched. Suddenly, a huge presence rose up over us, blanketing the sky, and no longer could I separate inside from out. The wings beat . . . the Presence grew . . . The dark, hovering mass of alien being threw a net of bondage out over our trembling souls and as the shrouded figure approached the apex of the hill where we stood, the wall shook and beneath us was no longer the city in slumber but an abyss of incalculable depth.

Darkness washed over us like the Nile in flood. We were tiny, atomized; droplets of water on an ocean of evil that poised itself for the downward plunge. Then—like the moment of calm in a hurricane's eye—came stillness, and Ariane's voice somewhere on the wind, calling, "Choose! Choose!" I lashed out, desperate, and found myself clutching a spar of wood—crossed like a T and bleeding onto my hands. Somewhere, somebody screamed.

The darkness was alive. I was drowning in it.

Then the elements resolved and these were left:

The footsteps . . . the figure . . . the abyss yawning . . .

And Walker beside me, still gasping, but saying again, "You're an angel. Make it stop," and this time I knew he wasn't looking at me. A light shaft lit my brain, crossed itself and encircled my chest like a belt. Dimly . . . still drowning in the darkness . . . I felt the furred wings retreat.

There were no more footsteps. I looked behind me. There was no shrouded figure. No movement at all on the hill above the sleeping town. Just Walker gibbering, and me.

Then my eye caught movement again. Beyond us this time, where a yellow mist encircled the street lamp and a faint odor of burning jasmine drifted up from the fog. Preening on the wall was a cat. A one-eared orange tom whose back arched and twisted—and a moment later, was gone.

I let go my grip on the wall and turned around to lean against it. My hands were cut and throbbing. There was a taste of blood inside my mouth and somewhere I could still smell the Presence, rotten and malign, but retreating at last.

"An angel," said Walker, but after that he fell again to gibbering.

## XV

We walked on through the night, still heading out of town. My body felt bruised from the inside out and I was sure Walker was worse, but movement was all we could manage. When Walker tried to talk it was nonsense, sheer babble, so we stepped it off in silence, along the terraced rowhouses of Bristol's working class. Across street after street after faceless street. No lights in the houses. No cars or buses. Just four slapping feet on quiet pavements. Past Horfield and Downend, out beyond the city zoo. Past the suburban fringe of sleeping commuters in their tidy bungalows. Walking wounded. Not talking, not thinking. Heading east . . .

Walking toward the light.

Eventually we went back to the flat. It took every bit of nerve the two of us possessed, and if there'd been another way out we'd have used it. But we'd left behind not only our shoes, but our packs and sleeping bags, our passports, our maps and all.

It was nearly noon when we stood again on the pavement looking up at the doorway where we'd last seen Ike. An old man shuffled past us, head down and limping, with the smell of sour cheese clinging to his overcoat. He pulled a metal shopping cart stuffed high with scraps of paper and empty boxes and I envied him. I truly did. He didn't have to climb those steps.

Just inside the hallway was a dried pool of red that matched the crusted blood on Walker's feet. As we stepped across it, into the room beyond, I saw him twitch—once, then twice again—in long shivers that ran the length of his left arm.

Chas was still on his pillow throne, glassy-eyed and staring at the wall. Most of the others were gone. I don't know what we'd have done if the lady in red had been there. Ike must have heard us enter, because he came out of a back room, wrapping a kimono around him. Just for a moment, his face was clouded by some emotion, but then he shoved it deep and treated us to another slinking smile. "What'll it be?" he said. "Tea? A joint? Three packets of Smarties?" Walker's grunt was the only reply.

We moved fast, chucking everything into the packs for later sorting. Ike circled behind us in the room, straightening ash trays, re-shelving books—and humming a tune that caught in the back of my throat. Chas had contrived to sit on the edge of my woolen sweater, but when I said, "Mind moving?" he never replied. Never even budged. I gave a tug, and then another, and as the sweater came free Chas toppled sideways and lay with his head resting on a pair of spike-heeled boots, still glassy-eyed and not moving at all.

I looked around, but Walker hadn't noticed. He was heading barefoot for the landing door. I followed, but when Ike said, "You haven't seen the cat, have you? He's disappeared," I looked back, thinking to comment. What I saw shut my mouth right quick. It was Maggie, framed in the doorway of the room that held the locked trap door where Walker and I had fled futilely for the roof. Her hair was chopped and frizzled, as if the barber had used a hatchet and a match. Her mouth was open, but nothing came out except drool. She looked a thousand years old.

I put my hand on the door and fled.

## XVI

FOR A WHILE AFTER THAT, I just figured Walker needed time. The distrust he showed in his eyes whenever I caught him looking at me was unsettling in the extreme, but I knew all too well how jarred my own psyche had been. Who could blame him for taking longer?

We hitched back into London and took up residence in an "official" crash pad—15p a night and all the bugs you could kill. There were over a dozen of us in the bigger dorm. Women with kids, tramps, a few junkies; even two gay blades who slurped so loudly after lights out that they were eventually given a separate room. Mostly, Walker lay on his bunk. He wouldn't talk to me at all about the West Country trip. I bought a second-hand Bible from a stall in the Portobello Road and fell to marking passages. Every now and again, I'd read out a piece to Walker, but it only seemed to scare him more.

Then Celeste showed up and Walker's problems took a back seat. She and I split London and headed north, to Scotland. For the first few days, we were like wild deer, ready to bolt at the first sign of contact. We talked over, under, and around what really mattered, exploring emotional territory as if we were animals returning to the forest after a fire: probing delicately at once-familiar ground, wondering if life could return to the charred remains.

"I had a dream," Celeste said once, when we were standing on a hill outside Edinburgh, looking across at the Firth of Forth.

"You always have a dream. You dream enough for any ten people."

The wind was whipping her hair across her face and she looked like an Arab, veiled against the day. "This was different," she said. "It wasn't like my usual dreams. It felt . . . it felt more like I was dreaming for you."

I started to say something glib, but the moment didn't feel right.

"It was like I was chasing you," she said, "even though I didn't want to." She cleared the hair back out of her eyes. "And a wind was blowing, blowing hard, and as fast as I went, the wind would blow you further away. There was a lake, and a cave—or sort of a grotto—and hallways that led to a pit. I kept chasing and you kept running. I didn't even know why."

She'd moved in close to me, there on the hillside, and for the first time in weeks we were touching tight enough to share our warmth. "I kept calling," she said. "But I wasn't sure I was calling the right name. And then, just for a moment, I saw you close by and I was sure I'd caught you up."

"And so you did," I said, and dared to put my arm around her.

But she shook her head. "No, it wasn't like that. You held up your arm, like this, and your hand was bloody. And in your hand was . . . was a piece of wood or something, and it was bleeding too."

The wind blew cold along my back and I pulled her closer still, wrapping us together like skin on bone. "I thought you were restless last night," I said. "But I know where you got that. It was from me telling you about the day on the Tor."

Celeste kept her eyes fixed on the water channel, plunging eastwards to the sea. "It wasn't last night, Michael. I had that dream in Spain." She turned to face me briefly and then looked away. "It was the night I decided I had to return."

Around us, the wind swirled and gusted, blowing her hair 'til I lost myself in it, smelling again the scent of love.

## XVII

THAT WAS HARDLY THE END of it all, though somehow, it was the beginning of something new. Celeste and I went up into the Highlands, and when we came back we were lovers again. It was time to go home.

I kept that Bible busy even when we landed back in the States. Celeste wasn't too interested, but I did pin her down long enough to talk about the parable of the rock and the sand, and which house crumbled when the storm waves beat upon it.

Mostly, she let me go, and we both found new roads to travel—some alone and some together. It took weeks for her to understand what had happened in Bristol and years before she got over the fear of having me wake up, shouting aloud the name of the Lord, because I'd been visited again in sleep by a manifestation of the awful Presence.

Walker drifted on in his own dream. It was months before our paths crossed again and by then, as I should have seen, it was already too late. His distrust of my role in the events in Bristol had hardened into the cold clay of certain fear. The simplest acts had become impossible for him: ordering breakfast; choosing a route; tying his shoes. On good days his hand barely twitched at all, but on others his entire arm jittered and shook, as if he were buffeted by a wind no one else could feel. He held a few jobs briefly, but after he was fired twice in two weeks—from a custodial temp service and a potato chip factory—he moved back in with his mom, and nobody heard from him at all.

I tried calling a few times. Even went out to the old homestead to see him, but he wouldn't come to the door. Or couldn't. Once I heard a rumor that he'd married, but it wasn't true. He just disappeared. Celeste and I went on. In time, even the visitations stopped and I thought I was free of it all.

Then, years after, I saw Walker unlocking a bicycle from the stand outside the courthouse . . .

From above the Wabasha Bridge, the Mississippi dissolves into a grey-green mist as I blink back the tears. Best friend I'd ever had. If I were Catholic, I would cross myself. Instead, I cross the street. Walker's bike is a speck in the sunset and the big river rolls on beneath the bridge. There is not a hint of darkness.

# ACKNOWLEDGEMENTS

The following stories have been previously published (all publications in USA except where noted):

"Song for a Road Partner," *Ellipsis*, Vol. 27, No. 1, Fall 1990

"In the House of Mr. Poo," *Glimmer Train*, Issue 6, Spring 1993; *Iron Magazine* (England), Issue 70, Summer 1993; *Horizon* (Belgium; in Dutch translation) Issue 99, September 1996; *Takahe* Magazine (New Zealand), Issue 29, January 1997

"The Road Goes Ever On," *Wascana Review* (Canada), Vol. 17, No. 2, Fall 1983 (as "Partners of the Road"); *Horizon* (Belgium; in Dutch translation) Issue 102, Winter 1997-98; *Takahe* (New Zealand) 34, August 1998

"The Man on the Train," *Four Quarters*, Vol. 32, No. 3, Spring 1983; *Detours II*, Lonesome Traveller Publishing (Canada), 1998

"Dust to Dust," *The MacGuffin*, Vol. XVIII No. 2, Special Issue, 2001

"Unto Us, the Spoils," *Raritan,* Vol. XXXIII, No 3, Winter 2014

"Waiting for the Void," *Island* (Australia) Issue 109, Winter 2007

"Sometimes," *Pearl 46*, Fall 2012

"Jumping Off," *Wellspring*, Summer/Fall 1993 (as "The Country of the Blind")

"Grandfather and the Fish-Glove," *Elysian Fields Quarterly*, Vol. 11, No. 4, 1992; *Studio* (Australia), No. 67, Winter 1997

"A Touch of the Word," *Hometown Press*, Spring 1989; *Wellspring*, Summer 1989; *The Family*, Sept. 1991; *Imago* (Australia), Summer 1997; *Cambrensis* (Wales) No. 37, 1998

"The Boots of Alfred Bettingdorf," *Identity Lessons*, Penguin, NY, 1999; *Studio* (Australia) No. 78, Autumn 2000

"A Rocker's Guide to the History of the Future," *Iron Magazine* (England) No. 52, 1987

"The Watcher," *Hamline Journal,* 1997; *Takahe* (New Zealand) Issue 33, April 1998; *Cambrensis* (Wales) No. 43, Spring 2000

"The Devil Don't Sleep 'Til Sunrise," *Iron Magazine* (England), Issue 63, 1991; *The Wolf Head Quarterly,* Vol. 2, Issue 1, Autumn 1995

"By the Terebinths of Mamre," *The Wolf Head Quarterly* Vol. 1, Issue 2, Winter 1994

## ABOUT THE AUTHOR

Daniel Gabriel's published work includes a novel (*Twice a False Messiah*), a short story collection (*Tales From the Tinker's Dam*), and hundreds of nonfiction articles, in addition to serving as editor for *Punch at the Wild Tornado*, a COMPAS anthology of student writing. For more details, check out http://danielgabriel.us.

Gabriel is also a lifelong vagabond traveler who has traveled by camelback, tramp freighter, and third class trains through over 100 countries, often with his wife Jude and sons Alex and Evan. En route, he worked as an English teacher in Spain, an apple picker in the Alps, a sailor in Scandinavia and the West Indies, a publican in Wales, and a roadie for Sly & the Family Stone, among other endeavors. Gabriel holds an MA in Cross-Cultural Studies from Fuller Theological Seminary and is currently statewide Arts Program Director for COMPAS.

## ABOUT NEW RIVERS PRESS

New Rivers Press emerged from a drafty Massachusetts barn in winter 1968. Intent on publishing work by new and emerging poets, founder C. W. "Bill" Truesdale labored for weeks over an old Chandler & Price letterpress to publish three hundred fifty copies of Margaret Randall's collection, *So Many Rooms Has a House But One Roof.*

Nearly four hundred titles later, New Rivers, a non-profit and now teaching press based since 2001 at Minnesota State University Moorhead, has remained true to Bill's goal of publishing the best new literature—poetry and prose—from new, emerging, and established writers.

New Rivers Press authors range in age from twenty to eighty-nine. They include a silversmith, a carpenter, a geneticist, a monk, a tree-trimmer, and a rock musician. They hail from cities such as Christchurch, Honolulu, New Orleans, New York City, Northfield (Minnesota), and Prague.

Charles Baxter, one of the first authors with New Rivers, calls the press "the hidden backbone of the American literary tradition." Continuing this tradition, in 1981 New Rivers began to sponsor the Minnesota Voices Project (now called Many Voices Project) competition. It is one of the oldest literary competitions in the United States, bringing recognition and attention to emerging writers. Other New Rivers publications include the American Fiction Series, the American Poetry Series, New Rivers Abroad, and the Electronic Book Series.

Please visit our website newriverspress.com for more information.